INTO THE GATEWAY

PREDATORS' KINGDOM

CLADENNIS U. DE LEON

Into the Gateway

tellwell

Tellwell Talent
www.tellwell.ca

ISBN
978-0-22888-340-1 (Hardcover)
978-0-22888-339-5 (Paperback)
978-0-22888-342-5 (eBook)

TABLE OF CONTENTS

PROLOGUE

Has it ever crossed your mind, even in a split second the notion that those ancient remnants of carved rock structures and walls with a gateway-looking feature possess a hidden manipulation to get through them? What if they were made that way, to look like it's a dead end, but the secret lies in sketched codes hiding in plain sight in the vicinity? Or could it be that a secret 'keeper' exists but pretends to know nothing of it until guaranteed to have no choice but to stop the discoverer by any means for the reason to better sacrifice a few rather than putting the millions into vulnerability?

Fear-provoking or mind-captivating, a gateway is a gateway until what lies beyond crosses it!

I became a supernatural while growing up in England. My curiosity that led my innocence to a tragic accident has opened up my keen insight with the power to see what isn't evident to the average mind, that the biosphere we live in as a planet is full of networking mystery, gateways to another World, yet perhaps a kind of device to hold boundaries between and among worlds.

However, to the posthuman Zenie's critiquing mind it's the Congregation of the Elders of brotherhood with the Deadly who imposed domineering oppression to hold boundaries of hierarchy among Brotherhoods.

That's why some incantations, whisper orations, and alchemy prayers are forbidden or forever hidden, only persuaded under endowment officially. That is why if Elder Brother says no to risk, it's a NO!!!

But in some ways, curiosity kills the cat.

"Early 19th century, the year 1830 when I was born in England where agricultural procures progress to British rivaled to other European countries. As I get older farming declined, and America gains better because of its ingenuities and inventions, steamboats to name one of them. But Europe has something better, we don't want the world to know, the Philosopher's Stone (a black monolith fragment from the World of Deadly), and by the power of the alchemy to open gateways to another World, we are far more up to the minute than any continent in the planet, we just want the world to know it as a myth except for us..."

"Nothing unscientific to a father furnishes greatness when it implies a risk to his own son, despite how supernatural or divine the risk it might be."

-Zenie Boy

CHAPTER ONE

BEWARE!!!

Agility, hypersensitivity, scorching. These characterized the carbonizing of the skin when exposed to UV radiating sun causing agonizing transformations, and that's why only the unstoppable bolting towards the dark forest diminishes the pain and the continuous inevitable shedding off my charred superficial skin.

"It stings a lot all over my body, the burning sensation, I'm like steaming!" And it seems I felt too vague to comprehend how I'm feeling. Right now, I'm both too exhausted and uneasy that I want to run fast... but to what direction...to where?

This confusion caused me to dash to random velocities where my steaming and aching jolting body prefers to bring me...at the very minute, I move onward but occupying miles of distances around thick woods already, in a blink of an eye, stampeding on wild animals... bruising them, some decapitated, and some died on the spot. The speed is so uncanny knack, I am supposed to see my shadow on the ground following me, but even myself seemed to disappear in my sonic speed, the only thing I remember are those specks of dust that appear to be time-stopped, meaning I swiftly move in a fraction of seconds until I crashed into something.

The pain really gripped every possible synapse as I mumbled to myself.

"Beware of your astonishing (cough)...ah it hurts... power and strength!" In disgust, I blamed a protruding branch that has stabbed my shoulder. Grimacing and crying out the pain so loud, **my agonizing cries are words to my ears but weren't words to a human who can hear,** they were loud howlings and roars of a monster repeatedly! My mind recollected how my parents worry that instant about my distressing situation. "Bloody I had turned into posthuman!"

My parents couldn't withstand seeing what I'd become. Who wouldn't feel anxious and stressed but classified to them I know I can endure any form of trauma...even hoping so in the long run.

The father who was stressed that his boy was away was readying himself to follow him to where he assumed the boy was going, to the log cabin until he heard that howling. He hastens to leave the house and that howling he's certain was his son's.

With culminating, mixed uncomfortable emotion, Mia (wife of Dr. Zendre Joshu) conveyed her anxious feeling, clasping both her hands together, "Is this really happening to our son?!" And the howling so loud reverberated throughout the woods. "What's that mean?" Asked the wife to her husband who barely could talk, but his actions and fussing gestures in silence compensate for his act, he's theorizing the first outcome. He's relating words mentioned during the previous weeks by his old friend at work, "there will be more howling, beware and take precaution to distance yourself."

Trembling from the inside out, he wishes to stop it and calm himself down by holding on to something, that's why he looked at his wife, regretting in overflowing tears, he embraced her who desperately wanted to know the whereabouts of their son.

"Ssshh... (hugged her tight) I'm worried, too...you can feel that. For Zenie to take an overwhelming transformation, the consequences that I imagine, are too painful and heartbreaking."

She dried her tears, but they kept flowing on her cheeky face...and offer herself to come and help to search with him. "There's no need Mia, I want you to stay home safe and lock all doors and windows, just promise me...don't come out."

He assured his wife he would not be alone...

"I will get help from Elder Brother, this old man can deal with our son's situation better. According to him, our son would turn into something much more intelligent and with a speed, not even our eyes can cope up... the old man said, he's not a werewolf, much farther on... than a werewolf!"

I was stuck! This branch has pierced through my shoulder, groaning as I decided on one option although it added more pain to my stinging body, to slowly pull out myself as I back off. I kept groaning, and my tears flowed incessantly. I sound like a dog whining due to aggravating pain. To add up to my stress-provoking situation, I just heard incoming like two people coming in my direction, when one of them clumsily stepped on a twig...its snapping break reaches my full attention. I thought of another option to get loose from this annoying prick on my shoulder. Quickly I swipe the obstinate sturdy branch of the trunk with my claws...without hesitation, I took out the remaining branch...with my strong gripping hand. I immediately climbed up a tree, hiding in the deep branches.

They came to my location and spotted some of my evidence as they rigorously inspect as to what creature it belonged to.

"Look! A scratch mark of a big animal, still fresh...perhaps a grizzly!"

The taller guy had inspected the tree and he doubted, shook his head... looked down for other clues. "I would believe so, but I noticed different bizarre footprints. I don't think it belongs to a grizzly."

"We need to have a bigger weapon I supposed."

"For what? It could be a prank...there's no such thing as an animal with that crazy footprint! Nonsense, pal!" He laughed at the hideous facial reaction of his companion.

"I'm hungry...want to share some piece of your ration?"

"So am I, sooner or later today, we can find real meat food, and shelter...we just have to wait and roam the forest." Despite the hunger, while lingering in the woods, it's for their own good than blending into the nearby town which he had insight is more dangerous.

Glaring two red eyes in the dark. Panning above the two guys in my transformation, hiding and blending in the thick dark branches. As I clenched to the higher trunk by the support of my claws to steadily and stealthily hold up my weight, I watched over them as they move on.

I climbed down. I walk in the other direction...**I drifted away not because of fear of them, but the fear of something unavoidable.** Just noticed the wound through my shoulder has closed permanently, no idea how long that took, so I did a self-assessment experiment with my claws and slowly sketch them on my left upper limb. I counted in seconds like how my science teacher taught me, "one-one thousand, two-one thousand, three-one thousand..." And all the clean incised cuts close. "I can't imagine this is happening to me and my consciousness is fully aware beyond my capacity to adapt...what kind of adaptability is this within me, everything has been augmented to an enormous degree, my senses have evolved it seems, everything perceived around me became nuance despite irritable to my hearing...ahh...it's killing me...dad it's so overwhelming!"

I stop moving...look around me, there can be no one near up close but the sounds in my ears contradict the subtle distinction. I ran to where more vegetation can be found in the woods, the robust the better so I could lurk. Behind tall bushes, I cramped my shivering muscled body, wrapping it tightly with my father's cloak like I'm in the cold weather. The minutes became hours, and my adaptation began to collide with all perceived. I slowly loosen the plugging to muffle the sound and I felt everything has come parallel to my transformation.

I got up. Resume my walking. I don't even know what time it is. I remember I left home to hide, and mom got awakened because of me, of my uncontrolled and fated metamorphoses. It even gets me worse and hyper when I overheard dad on the way inside the house from his midnight shift work at the School of Alchemy and Wisdom. I remember I broke the doorknob getting out to drift away from anyone, after crushing my bed leaving behind sheds of burned skin, and a little scorch mark by the wall. With all those pieces of proof of my metamorphosis, can't blame them to get in a panic having no clue if I can manage to handle myself out here without concerning myself with precautions and hurting others, I knew nothing about metamorphosing myself and not knowing of its consequences whether it would turn out bad to me or to the people around.

Speaking of what time it is right now, I overheard from almost a thousand meters, between an old couple chatting on their way home from their orchard farm, disputing a little about being late and the old lady just uttered it's half an hour after five...besides hurrying up and had decided to pace up a little, I suddenly stopped...I saw the couple cease to walk in the middle of the dirt road, their heartbeat has altered into a fast pounding of fear, I knew them from two blocks away from our abode, owning a mini fruit and veggies stall...it's Mr. and Mrs. Brown.

"Did you hear that?" Asked the husband to Mrs. Brown, gesturing to her with an open hand to mean quit moving for a while. Mrs. Brown has presbycusis, an age-related hearing loss, and has complained for the past few months that she couldn't tolerate loud sounds. She acted to listen while vaguely looking in all directions squinting her brows. "What did you hear, exactly Jim?" The wife gets closer to her husband clenching slowly to his left arm. "Maria...I hear strong sneaking brushing against close by bushes," the old man never put more words to describe what that implies which only tells that there are multiple big predators around. He rested his small wooden wheelbarrow piled with two buckets full of fruits and veggies, and a couple of gardening tools. "Here... Maria. Throw some apples, the husband gives his wife one in each hand to equip her with something to scare them away once they would emerge, and he readied himself with a shovel.

"The fork is way better, Jim." The wife suggested as the husband quickly comply and replaced it with it.

With the panning view, my eyes could adjust...the beat of their pumping organs vividly appear so translucent, "what did I just do? Another adaptation of my instinct?" It seems unfamiliar to my sight, but I can view creatures with heat signatures, with the sound of the heartbeat heeds my echolocation. This is like the hunting view of one predator...to direct me to my target prey. I hid behind a tree, losing my mind but trying to fight it by finding the remaining human inside of me, input in my memories. Wrong timing and my stomach growled.

"I can tolerate this hunger, but their blood in their vein, I can smell the traces of their blood on their sweat glands." I was talking to myself but growling. The satiety to devour isn't my instinct to control, I must feed, **but there's my human nature still intact and instinctively alive trying to outweigh the predatorial instinct.** With my drool salivating from my fang that mutated obviously, I took a pinching bite on my muscled arm, I felt the oozing blood into my quenched dried throat and sighed...I did it!

Over-enthusiastic, unrestrained, clever, plotting and moving in smart! "I heard three big predators prowling... into the direction of the couple!"

That's the most logical reason I had seen denoting why Mr. and Mrs. Brown suddenly slowed down their walking pace and then stop.

At that very exact moment, advancing at an accelerated rate of three big wolves, I turned my face with my glowing glaring red eyes to where they are coming from, almost ten meters away from the old couple. Never expected that would come. I just heard them plotting, the three of them, to take down the couple for their pack waiting to be fed deeply into the woods. "What's this instilling into my keen insight?!"

"Bloody hell, first time to hear wilds communicate. That I didn't see it coming, I could comprehend how these wilds talk in their growls and snarls." My heart pounded before because of fear out of precaution, but NOW... it's because of necessity! I can hear the three wolves are going to ambush and kill the two starting first with the lady...and I swoosh with my speed!

I move in to intervene, not the motion the three wolves expect but the unparalleled interruption these smart guys never had expected in their entire life, I saw their attacking scene very sluggish in my red glaring eyes, all of them are in slow motion but me running, leaping, and with my wide grab all three of them were caught in my vantage. The whiplash I created didn't hurt them as I did a thorough scouring of my *Thermo* vision showing no sign of internal bleeding or fractures in them. I made sure they landed on me rather than hitting themselves on a hard tree trunk, sticking out branches, and prickly uneven ground surface. My quick eye reflex has served accurately to locate where each is going to smash into. Glad I had to cushion them! They just have suffered shock from the unexpected and humiliation, and I could justify that because we are in partial commune understanding their thoughts and hurt gestures after the incident.

As expected, we stood up slowly to get back to awareness, their pinch snarling upper lips began to express specific views they want to convey not just infuriation, asking me for some clarifications.

The alpha verifying. "Who are you to be in our way hunting food?"

One companion seconded. "Yeah, who are you...despite outnumbered, so foolish...arrogant not even hesitating in searching for a death wish..."

But when I stood up bipedally and saw whatever in me, they turned their back and try to drift away. I felt a bit guilty, their despair to hunt food was halted because of me.

"Hey stop there!" They understood my growls and roars, and they look back...the wife of the alpha called him, mumbling, "the red-eye monster wolf wanted to say something." The alpha walked closer ordering his companions to spread out, just in case. "Do you have something to say, make it quick."

"I am also like you...and I was also like them. Those two humans you wanted to become your prey; I cannot allow that! Not only because we knew each other, but because they aren't designed in the ecosystem to be your food."

"What about those humans who wanted to attack our clan, how would you defend us if you say you are like us?" The wife wanted to test the big creature's opinion.

"Diverse creatures including humans have one goal, to sustain oneself to survive, and that includes defending."

The alpha spoke but contradicted directly what was utterly explained by the big creature. He gestured to the other companion to excavate from the ground and show the proof. "They aren't defending, they have the projectile launcher that makes a loud sound and another with no sound but longer and has barb. They laughed at their content when these humans kill our kind. What would you suggest, if you say you are one of us?" The one companion came back in his snout holding an arrow and lay it on the ground, the proof.

"Not all humans are the same, that old couple you attempted to ambush are nice people. They live together just by themselves, treated people and animals whom they acknowledge friendly and not strangers, hospitably."

"I would run away and by chance, it's also in my nature to defend myself and my family and clan...if I need to. But remember this, there's always a choice as pre-attempt before you make up your mind whether to run or to fight...because sometimes worst scenario cannot be avoided."

For inquisition's sake, the alpha didn't hesitate to ask, despite the strong aura of my predatorial instinct, "what are you exactly? A humanoid wolf?"

"I'm guessing another species but not of a humanoid wolf or werewolf, my kind of clan does not exist nor linger around here, they're from another world but it's hard to explain."

"I have a shelter close by, a log cabin that's where I am going to hide away from people, I don't want them seeing me like this. Visit me when you have the chance."

One worst scenario is about to intercede during our conversation, a hunting knife is being thrown skillfully attempting a target, the wife of the alpha, but before the knife reaches her, a burst of aura around me manifested profusely. Stop the advancing blade with my swiping claws, the blade fragmented into three pieces, implicating the test resistance of the claws is beyond comparison.

The wolves didn't anticipate the lashing out onto the blade until three of its fragments scattered, one hit a tree, one went to the ground, and the other part ricocheted somewhere after hitting a rock.

"There are hunters!!! Run to the east, I have saved you food, a lot for your clan, go now and I will deal with these maltreaters!"

I hastily picked up one piece from the fragmented hunting knife and kept it for myself. Put on my Thermo vision seeing two coming my way; these were the guys who saw the scorch marks I made earlier.

The tall guy knew his knife throwing wouldn't have missed his target, but never heard any wolf grunt, he began to wonder. Coming back at him is the other guy who just went through if they'd wounded a wolf, "no single blood was spilled, mate."

He scoured and looked for his knife but can't find it anywhere in the vicinity, suspecting something weird, the tall guy prattled, "there's something anomaly going on in this wood," he mumbled to continue what he theorized from the fragmented blade's outcome. "I'm not hallucinating despite this hunger, but only a fool believes in ghosts." He suddenly moves to hide from a tree, like somebody is in pursuit of them while telling his mate to do the same who reacted weirdly and thought of him if he had smoked too much.

He started mumbling and along behind him followed his pondering mate who still couldn't get what was going on with his pal. **"Whoever you are...my mind is lucid even how long I have served in prison...treated like an animal!** I got bored I need to do something to escape. And as for you guardian of the woods, we will soon come to see each other face to face..."

They barely could see the path made by the fleeing wolves, that's what they thought and that's the only reason they're persistent in their pursuit of the known creatures but unaware of what they believed, they're coming after what is bigger and unknown. The broken twigs, the trail of rapid running on the ground, but their insistent tracking suddenly stops!

"The trail of the wolves vanished! How's that possible?" Now they have no direction to rely on where they have gone, in what direction, and it's getting darker sooner. They look up at the big trees and there they saw the same scratches of the five big claws. The tall guy couldn't believe the same claws of five scorches is seen on a higher level of the tree.

"Another prank, boss?"

"Are we dealing with some kind of werewolves here?" And he tried to connect the collective clues behind, the unusual big footprints, the missing hunting knife, and then the scratch mark of tree bark twelve feet above them. "Werewolves can do that but only in comics, not in reality."

It's getting darker, no idea that a shelter made of logs is only a hundred meters away from them.

The three wolves that I met in the woods had come and visited me, had brought thigh meat of dear as I let them in for company.

"You're human after all, and no longer the red-eye giant wolf, and you look a fine young man to us." they came nearer and lick his face, a friendly rapport of actions made by predators to someone they give respect. Well, that's because Zenie is in his calm state, even his aura emits like everyone else just a plain simple normal guy. Zenie narrated how he obtain the transformation and became one of the kinds of apex predators that live in another World, "that if my kind would cross the gateway coming into our world, would they suffer the same agony that I had suffered this early morning? Would they respect animals in the wild and humans who cannot defend themselves with the swift motion I am adaptable to?"

I wonder how they live in their territory; do they need to be exposed to the daylight to transfigure into a big creature as I do?

CHAPTER TWO

THE REALM DOOR (PART 1)

Nine years ago...

It's a dark, very enigmatic, and risky subjugation that happened when I was six. That's my age era, the rebirth of European wisdom, somewhere in Midwest England had been organized supernatural organization of alchemists, the Brotherhood of Alchemy and Wisdom, *Black Canis lupus* region. But they aren't alone throughout Europe.

Out of purest love for my mother Mia Yeng, my father, Dr. Zendre Joshu, joined the Brotherhood of Wisdom and devoted himself to practicing science and medicine, differently, the forbidden occulting supernatural way despite ordained with left and right risks. He signed a covenant letter with the seal of his blood and bound ready to jeopardize his life as long as his despairing needs to heal his wife's suffering from cancer would be met.

I was very young, but I could feel if afflictions of sickness and burden affected my parent. Trying to sugarcoat, my mother lying in the hospital bed continued to lie about her health in front of me, but she isn't aware I was gifted at deciphering truth from lies. Father embraced me snugly, seemed like my mum's number is running out, and from there, father admitted that my mother got afflicted with ovarian cancer, a case during medieval times even rich families couldn't attempt to fight. Medical experts would rather choose to say it with gestures like a shake of their head signifying that my mom's case is hopeless, and I know mom would leave me soon, instead of me sleeping next to mom during thunderstorm nights on her beautiful soft mattress bed, there will be no more of her to appease me when I get scared.

Medical experts' assessment, she would not have lived for another year. Dad sought an old friend working in the Alchemy School of Wisdom, he's an older friend in the Wisdom of the Black Canis lupus, has resolved my father's anxiety, but the price to find the cure is deadly if recklessly done. Both deadly inside and outside the *realm door*, literally!

Realm door? It's the most forbidden thing in the World and the law of the Brotherhood of Wisdom of any region has restricted to put to use either one to obtain god powers from the three realm doors entering. The only exception to the rule is the 'realm endowment' because it's official. When the ritualistic realm endowment is practiced inside a hall in the Wisdom, it's because it's by the law to reward a brother with an everlasting gift, a power of either immortality (from plants), deadly magic (mineral gems), or a weapon to scavenge (from Predators' Kingdom).

But for unofficial, once caught and proven guilty, no other things will be disputed but to resolve the matter by the quote, pay what you owe, which means an exile into the realm door and be locked forever...or become the property of and of service to the Great Congregation.

Unofficial or self-doing of realm endowment would only endanger the person, or in some probable cases, a creature from the inside could cross the realm door making the human world into a vulnerable space.

Dr. Zendre Joshu cried his burden to one old friend, an alchemist. He knew he could trust him, not knowing the lofty rank the old friend holds in the Brotherhood of Wisdom, *midnight (the Black) Canis lupus* region, region of the black wolf. "With all the strength left in me and my will, I'd rather gamble with my life to save a family, especially when the person is someone you gain your source of power from the most." Said Dr. Zendre J.

The next night. Elder Brother dragged him by the wrist and took him down the spiral staircase heading down the deeper mazy dungeon. With the quartz torch, both grab each. Still, Elder Brother ignited each with his Luminaire eyes, an ancient ability passed on to the Brotherhood as their foundational power, the first power to be bestowed to each newbie.

"Here's a *small piece of the Black Monolith.* My grandfather's father gave it to him saying he obtained it through friendship across the gateway, he said one word... the Deadly.

"I believe I have it for a reason, and that reason is now...for your family's sake, I know you have a pure spirit to use it, use it at midnight, return it to me tomorrow, same time at this place. Remember Zendre, this isn't an official *realm endowment,* so please be very cautious. No one must know, not even your family."

There are some traces of questions and doubt in the mind of my father as observed by Elder Brother, so he continued explaining the details of *realm endowment.*

"*It* is the official inheriting of power by an official brother before parting from the service, yet it is always the agreement between the officiating Brother (the ranked Chief eldest usually called the *Elder Brother*) and the inheritor, the brother who's retired of the service."

At precisely twelve midnight, the officiating Brother, the eldest among them in the ten-year term service, will seal the hall, the phenomenon procedure taken from the deadly spell realm, the *Red Crystal Radiance.* Red Crystal obtained from the Deadly World of casting a spell, can ignite into a flame of red once energy from Luminaire eyes is released upon the stone. Red symbolizes sealing which means no exit and no entry. It all means to stop or to shut.

Next, twelve warriors surround in circle around the floor on which the inheritor will sketch his door. The twelve, including the officiating eldest, are equipped with various weapons only used during the endowment: double blade ax, swords, spears, bladed chains, and bow and arrow, and meteor hammer as the line of defense whenever dangers as realm creatures may come out the door. These weapons were forged and made in the kingdom of the three realms. And are passed on to generations of any twelve realm warriors. But among the three realms, the Predator's Kingdom tyrannizes the harshest and has the most unwelcoming outlook on humans. The Vampire Wolf clan leads the Predator's Kingdom to believe humans are naturally biased creatures.

Weapons made in the Predators' are the true power. They have some kind of the realm language marking inscribed that respond by glowing whenever realm doors have been opened, or any creature human or gods from any realm shows up with ugly intentions."

"Once the inheritor comes back, he would state the password back to the elder. Whether the inheritor is back or not, time to the human world is the limit, twelve minutes, but beyond that, although agonizing on both sides of the officiating and the inheritor, the realm door must be sealed... once the officiating picks up the stone, the red crystal light occupies the sketched door.

When the inheritor succeeded to come back alive within the time limit, the verification follows. To do that, the inheritor must pick up first the black stone on the sketch door from the floor; the realm door closes and returns it by finding the eldest among the twelve. Holding the black crystal stone in his hands crossed behind his back, he walks towards the officiating eldest. And state back the correct password that was stated to him before. A password could be anything known in the Brotherhood of Wisdom, their emblem, the full name of the Elder Brother, the full name of the inheritor, and so on.

The twelve warriors surrounding the realm door stand at ease until then, which concludes the ceremony is a success.

The instruction of getting into the Immortality kingdom continues. "At exactly twelve midnight tonight, draw a door shape on the floor using the black stone and put down the stone on one corner of the drawn door. It will open up a portal, a very dark gate."

"A gate to what, Elder Brother?"

"It is a gateway that can open up three realms: Immortality kingdom, Predators' kingdom, and the kingdom of the Deadly (magic). Each opens up to the length of time you finish drawing the door on the floor, make sure no one follows you, because if someone does, that someone out of curiosity might enter the next realm, either the predators' kingdom or the deadly magic."

"Get to the immortality, use clean vials with caps and collect water from any bloomed flowers. The door won't close to you, but while you're inside, the realm door alternates three openings with your drawing's time length. However, if someone or something will accidentally move the black stone from where it was originally placed, you will be doomed inside forever!"

"Now, let your wife drink the water you collected, have some if you want, and spare a little for me, too, for my specimen. Just in case, my friend. That's all I ask in return."

From the deep dungeon, all is quiet with only the sound of dripping water, and the footsteps of incoming members can be heard. The two wearing their thick dark-cloaked coat, with a sword on their waist, climbed up the spiraled staircase with each quartz torch as their source of light. The old friend (Elder Brother) is well respected among the members except for one, the next in rank and jealous of him, Brother Narija, who is more on suspicion to fault-find anything from anyone.

"Brother Narija, why have you come downstairs with no torch? *Luminaire eyes* are only for an emergency, and I don't see any signs of chaos around. You might get hurt when you stumble in the darkness, have at least a torch with you next time, take this instead and I am done anyway with my session of guiding our younger brother in the mazy dungeon."

Brother Narija took the torch that was handed over to him by Elder Brother. With pretension behind that grateful smile, he responded to his question. "I heard some footsteps, so I come to check; forgive me for interrupting the tour and instructions of the... our younger brother."

In the banquet hall, they welcome new recruits and celebrate a feast and drinks for everyone.

In the middle of the superior table facing all the newbie brothers, Elder Brother stood up with pride and honor, walking near a bronze cauldron containing a large red quartz stone. With his Luminaire eye, he ignited the red quartz procuring a radiance of dim red all around the banquet hall. And Elder Brother uttered the words, "I just sealed the room!" The newbies look all around the vicinity wall as the deadly magical seal crawls the wall's surfaces so no one from the outside or even evil forces can break into nor hear of what he speaks of for them.

With the keen eyes of father, he got astonished to wonder; he'd thought the work of the Red Crystal Radiance was amazing, defying his simple science mind. Brother Narija, simply acts quietly but deep within, his watchful gaze is on the new recruit, Dr. Zendre Joshu.

"We are more than teachers, we are more than doctors, we are more than law enforcers, but we keep all these gifts secret in this House of Wisdom, and in my governance, you swore by its power to keep it low-profile, so that you can blend to the human world."

"Remember, you can only use the gifts when I assigned you a mission!"

"We welcome you all! As the wisdom of the city, we are obliged to protect the inside and outside for the sake of humanity's safety and health. Inside this Brotherhood of Alchemy and Wisdom, we have set rules. Only when under emergency and disarray will I allow you, brethren, to overcome any obstacle upon encounter by requiring your gift bestowed on you. Whenever I sense some of the rulebreakers making unworthy use of their gifts when I was in your rank, I get distracted because of its annoying wave coming at me. Metaphorically speaking, like a watchdog, I can easily perceive an intruder, so loud and tingling in my auditory canal. Likewise, you are handed each with the official cloak you can wear inside, and outside if under an assigned mission. As I said, you cannot perceive any danger yet, but at the moment, your cloak will perceive that for you. The emblem of the Black Wolf Brotherhood ignites, glowing at the presence of danger that only originates from the realm door."

Elder Brother also called the eleven warriors whom Brother Narija is one. By name, each stands up in acknowledgment, they are entirely wearing the warrior attire in the event of the welcome night—dark cloak, beast headgear, blade weapons, either swords or axes, impenetrable gauntlet, and boots.

By those words of advice to the banquet in general, Brother Narija took it personally, but again without losing his composure to brothers around him. He knew exactly that whenever the forbidden collections down the darkest locked dungeon had been broken into with the use of a brother's gift, punishable by the congregation's decision may follow.

That night, my father seriously transpired the ritual. I know how he wanted my mother to get well and be normal, to have a full life and love from her family; he's the one taking care of her daily needs without even hiring maids to do the chores. That's why father took a night shift to the Brotherhood of Alchemy and Wisdom.

Father has an office library den, where...he faultlessly sketches the black stone fragment of the Monolith on the wooden floor and places it on one of its corners...at first skepticism lingers in his thought, and from there when the floor has altered to an opening of another world, it was dimmer than his room so his eyes' pupils dilated...but tongue-tied, he couldn't fathom that there are crucial tools that can defy calculations and science.

His eyes grew with much awe, had just realized, **"my primitive knowledge is nothing compared to the new acknowledged application of an ancient tool!"**

But before everything else, he tucked me into bed and dressed up for his shift. After I became aware from my half-sleep, for I heard my door creak, I slowly but fearlessly opened my eyes, my room is totally dark, and I waited until it was fully adapted to it. However, I felt someone is home besides mom and me because I didn't really have my door closed after my father said goodnight. I heard someone slowly close my door and got awakened by it. Now I could see my entry, and it was shut; hearing someone walking away down the hall as I saw the candlelight fade out. I knew father said he was leaving to work, but he was supposed to be out hours ago.

Although I knew ahead, I didn't have light to guide me, I snuck up into the darkness; it never bothered me. Only a bad guy could... lurking in the dark. But at that age, I preferred to catch in the act whoever had trespassed into our house. I saw candlelight flickering through my father's office den's door on the floor. My heart started pounding as I near my ear on it. Not even one clattering of my father's stuff I haven't perceived. Why so quiet? That drives me to be more curious, but ironically, my stealthy move had accidentally pushed the door; it wasn't, after all, locked.

When I stepped in, my right foot step-hold on onto the pajama pants which unprevented slinging my full weight against the opened door; my age justified how clumsy I was. Fortunately, there wasn't anybody inside or my father whose hands and smile readily offered to take my hand and let me stand.

That's the moment I recklessly was introduced to the power of the fragment of the Black Monolith (the Philosopher's stone). It can open another world, where I got drawn to it. At first, when I crawled near it, it looks like a hole on the floor that was miter-cut by my father, that if I decided to get into, I would fall into an abyss because the other world in the opening is upsidedown. I was staring at tree branches as if I were lying on my back.

On the wooden floor where I was crouching, I see clearly the edge of the opening and after carefully inspecting around it, there's a newly encountered sitting stone on the corner. I took the stone from its place, the floor went back, and the open door vanished, only leaving the scratch drawing of the alchemy door on the floor. I realized it was the scratching sound made that I heard while getting off my bed.

After analyzing how it works, I put it back on the floor in its original spot. The door opens up again. I ran back to my room to put on my shoes, then randomly got into the opening. As I got into the realm door, my father came back but totally he was unaware of where I was. Even at the first encounter of that kind of sorcery of opening a doorway, has never given me how it works, all I thought was I could surprise to see my father on the other side telling me all about the sketch door.

In my new world, it only just starting to get dark. But I can tell it's a thick forest, but that didn't look like how I knew about woods when my father and I walked the trail to cross the woods to reach other towns. The woods where I was, looked colossal, and I assumed that any beasts in the area were also huge. I know it was getting darker, and as I said, darkness didn't bother me at all. I went back fifteen steps to where the door I had left; I was still tired, and I needed to go back. My situation instilled panic in me after knowing the door was gone. I couldn't track back my steps because I didn't bring any lantern with me, but based on my distance measurement, the door that led to my home must be around me...I know I am not mistaken.

But the wavering and finding of the realm door didn't give him much of his expectation, and his long waiting and wondering turned into some more horrific. He had experienced the perception of something's presence but couldn't identify what could be around, he knew something in the dark is watching over him, and once encountered a streak of red glow. He was snatched from behind, a big jaw that gripped his shoulder, he had the chance to catch a glimpse of the strong beast, but his fear of the encounter shut him to unawareness and unconsciousness. Zenie boy was dragged like a rag doll farther from the original spot where the realm door had emerged...but unaware to both the beast and the boy, the realm door emerges again.

CHAPTER THREE

THE REALM DOOR (PART 2)

Father just got out from the realm door with the feat in his hand, knowing that he's at the edge of the glory! He rushes with much gratitude and is fervently vigorous to see his wife, waking her up to have a sip on the vial.

But when it's time to get to my bedroom to tell me the good news, he's expecting I was sound asleep, but it's empty. He yelled out my name with a grin on his face very eager to tell me that my mom will live again fully as she is before. He waited so he leaned his back on the side of my bed, to think that he could surprise me when I gets back from the bathroom, thinking I am taking too long, he called my name the second time but still no response at all until the smile turns to scary worries. The silence is intolerable, swept the entire house, but nowhere to be found, and he just recalled what Elder Brother said when performing the ritual. "No one must be around so nobody would accidentally get into the opened realm door!" After the recall, his heartbeat races into the turbulence of life and death inevitability.

He scoured my room once again, under the bed, and inspected that my shoes were gone; it only means that I went somewhere, "my boy must have followed me into the realm door, but which realm did he go?"

Blaming himself, he promptly went back to his office den, and open the gate again by placing the stone where it initially stayed before. As the door opens, he has no idea which realm to check first, but he must do it hastily. Time is crucial but he knew I must have entered one of the two kingdoms randomly, the Deadly or the Predators' because he thought if I have gone to the same kingdom as where he is then we should have met.

Dr. Zendre Joshu has no clue what to do once he's inside the next kingdom to be in transpose. It's the Deadly! The howling wind and intermittent thunderclap are perceptibly loud and every time sparks of thunder skip through, entities of malevolence in shadows and silhouettes awaited him to step into. At first glance of the inside, a very striking disgust painted his face! He was about to enter when his wife halted him from his back, holding his shoulder. Mia is calm, unlike Dr. Zendre who is tense turned to face his wife expecting he might get a specific answer from her. Zendre saw the glow in her face looking at the next kingdom that has transposed inside the realm door, she pointed at it. It's the Predators' kingdom.

One thing for sure that awakened my father back to his awareness was a query in his mind. "How did my wife know which kingdom to enter?" And he realized the full vial of the immortal water that he let her drink. "You can find our boy, just focus Zendre, focus!" That's the voice of my mother, heard from his back when he entered, but the truth, mother was never there, it was only conjured up by father, so a mind whisper called, and it even eventuated twice.

Into the predators' kingdom, he roamed the colossal forest, it isn't actually the heart of the kingdom where most of the inhabitants of that kingdom live, but it's their hunting ground. Considering the random selection of where the sketched realm door is situated, it's so unfortunate timing that I have roamed the very place where predators hunt for their food.

It's the afternoon dark, father turned around and caught a sunset, and to the opposite that still reflects the remaining yellow golden radiance of the twilight outlines the highest peak that is shaped like a howling wolf. The cedar trees are triple the thickness and their height, but while he walks underneath those wide branches, he knew he was being watched from above.

"I can hear the snarling of the beast somewhere but not emerging. Its crackling sound of growl from low going high kills my spirit... I take my step very slowly. Whatever it takes, whatever it may cost me if one of us must survive and gets back through the realm door, it's you...Zenie boy!"

And from twenty steps straight he saw bloodstain on the ground, he followed what he thought looked like crawling marks or dragging marks that belongs to a young boy. He hoped it isn't a dragging mark. Near the lake beach, he saw me lying prone. He checked my limbs, all intact... and quickly pulsated me.

"He's alive! I prayed that I would find you...I did, I hope that you are alive...and you are," However, my abrasions on the chest and bite marks on my shoulder are making him lose his mind...he sobbed. "I'm going to get you out of here!" And he took a good gaze at the open realm door... preparing...focusing!

He turns around and runs towards the door. Beats of his pounding heart played like percussion drumbeats. Despite being aware that one beast is after him, he just doesn't have much care except for me to get through that door. His genius multi-tasking carries on with planning to sideswipe the stone once they're both in. Giant six feet tall, clawed creatures have sniffed the scent of human flesh, with luminary eyes in the dark, and the escaping humans have attracted more ambush. The beasts' glowing eyes seem to show flame-like when they're on the move! With that perceived motion witnessed by his peripheral vision, he knew certainly the creatures are supernatural. That being thought, he could assume humans like him couldn't outrun them. "I could just reach that door a little bit closer, and I will toss my son, no need to save myself, just reach out to swipe off the stone and stay put not to let the beasts get through me, final plan has made up my mind."

The moment he saw the alchemy door, he just... dived into it, risking whatever protrusive bones of his might have been fractured; he rolled hurting his hand as he heard the fractured sound, caught a glimpse of the stone, and forcefully kicks it. One big, clawed hand has gotten through while the door is shut! He's still in his unimaginable fall position on the floor when he heard a thudding on the floor; it's a decapitated huge humanoid wolf's right whole hand claw.

My shirt was soaked with my blood. He put me in a sitting position on my bed to slow down the bleeding and let me sip from the vial, despite my unconsciousness. He monitors my pulse. The wound stops bleeding. My consciousness has regained but is still a little bit dazed. The entire night he keeps his watch on whimpering. "I will not give up on you, take all the water and drink, just live...just live, please my son, live for your father...please?"

He inspected the four clawed scratches on my chest and the bite mark on my shoulder. The open wounds are healing in a manner defying normal process and time. The phenomenon was unbelievable, but he all saw it happening. The wounds have healed in just minutes.

He looks at the remaining liquid portion in the vial, wondering what components it is made of. "Can I make a synthetic copy through the science of alchemy of this liquid? Is it possible?"

As soon as he knew the water from the Immortal kingdom had healed the fresh wound, his tears started flowing profusely. Hugging me, he uttered, "I won't let you get away from my sight if ever I make some science ritual or weird experimentations next time."

He went back to his office to wrap everything left up, especially the sketched mark door on the floor. He wanted to erase the door mark with tools permanently, but no time, instead cover it with woolen carpet, picked up the stone, sealed it in a dark pouch, and kept it in his cloak's pocket. While looking at his untended broken wrist, he caught a stare on the floor of the decapitated wolf's hand claw. He put on some leather mitt and pick it up, sealed the hand claw in a big lab jar with a glass cap.

Nine years later...every day was a brand-new day for Dr. Zendre Joshu and his family, but not for the entire town. Two wanted kidnapped-for-ransom burglars had escaped the city's Victory prison. Zenie, growing up as a teenage boy, has never been easy, to pretend is hard, hardest when pretending to become just like an average kid, but he isn't anymore. Little by little his skills to do a single simple task can be learned in a day instead of normal one whole month. The school became boring to him and dissimulating just to disguise an action for the sake of the family's safety is what his father's advice to him. He remembered how Elder Brother briefed them saying to keep a low profile on matters that are divine or supernatural or else the Brotherhood of the Congregation will get startled and take control of the Brotherhood of the Black Wolf and their school of Alchemy and Wisdom.

Zenie's perceptions of things and occurrences are many steps ahead of him, thus, a great help to advantage to escape both dangers and threats. He also has visions. In fact, the two burglars are very clear in his head, seeing them face to face, so with their names, Tom, the taller guy, and Frank, the gullible. So, he directly pursued the scene in his vision and wherever the two wanted convicts unleashed their burglaries, Zenie could see them committing...in consciousness.

But there's more than meet the eyes. Father has invited Elder Brother for dinner, it's my fifteenth birthday, primarily to ask another favor from him, it's the eagerness to confess two things: my remarkable abilities and one weird, decapitated specimen. If not for the emerging unbelievable mind powers I disclosed, father wouldn't have bothered to call Elder Brother and reveal it.

"There's something I needed you to know but I kept it secretly for long while, for the reason that I'm afraid you would excommunicate me from the brotherhood."

And he brought out the big jar with the specimen soaked in formalin. Upon witnessing a beast's hand with those claws with a V-mark, the atmosphere of Elder Brother has altered to vigor spirit. Still holding the jar and placing it on the table, the old man brought out a locket from his inner shirt and exposed a red gem that mysteriously glistened.

"Shut all doors and windows, quickly!" He uttered a Latin and Enochian; the red gem emitted a glow to the entire chamber that sealed it from its original time.

"I understand why you delayed your irresponsible confession about the incident, I'm not mad at you. The fact that it has helped you and our Brotherhood in secret and safety from the Congregation, you know brother Narija is hard-headed and suspicious."

Elder Brother took his chance to check up on my scars. "Ah...Zendre, could you play happy music for the occasion, it's your son's birthday, we must celebrate with cheers." The sound is just to conceal what they are about to discuss concerning me. "Let me see your scar, boy..." Realizing the amount of scar, he knew how the immortality sap had helped heal my wound, "and your father said you experience high perception abilities like you know what's going on to your neighbor next door without even being there...astonishing and interesting, Zendre!" He nodded in belief.

"I'm afraid I can only define the creature who attacks your son, like the V-mark on their claws, they are clans or species of the apex predator ...unless there's a sample fresh enough to study for my research." The answer to his request was brought out when a cryopreserved tissue and blood of the creatures were handed over to Elder Brother in an individualized vial.

"Remember there's nothing to talk out of it regarding this matter."

It was explained to Dr. Zendre Joushu that the predators with the V-mark are the fastest and most intelligent beasts in the realm of predators. He explained to Zendre that they are clever and will not finish their prey to lure others, baiting them to come to save the victim. Zendre recalled when he took his son out of the predator's kingdom.

In the following days, Elder Brother permitted Dr. Joshu to be in his research lab and office.

"The Book of Three Realms pertains to the three kingdoms: the Immortality, the Predators, and the Deadly. Anywhere in the world using the Philosopher's stone aka in ancient terms called Fragment of the Black Monolith if sketched on the floor to make an alchemy door shape would open to any three kingdoms. And from the information assessed from your son, it matches the description of perception abilities because he had been bitten... by a Vampire wolf."

"What!? What's going to happen to my son?" The panic in his teary eyes began to shroud his perceptions.

"I know how exactly scary that sounds like, but with more science and info, we can both handle this...besides we both benefit from knowing all perspectives."

After the realm door incident confession, every night before everyone else in the Wisdom is about to nod off, Elder Brother and my father sneak up and snoop in the lab, and carefully experimented with the specimens' blood inoculated to mice in several attempts. Until the outcome has emerged, their working theory has been finalized.

"Metamorphosis, a transformation of creature or species at a stage where younghood and adulthood transpose, more aggressive changes would start to show. He becomes one of them. This means, that if he goes out in the sun, skin would be charred easily and shed off. His physical body expands, he would grow long hair in a minute. With the size of the hand claw, I'm guessing he would turn as huge as six to eight feet tall."

"Like a werewolf, Elder Brother?"

"Werewolves are just peripheral in contrast to Vampire Wolves."

"Let me continue. The intense burning sensation would aggravate the satiety to bolt and hurt someone, with the agility and strength of one strike with those long sharp claws, human or animal flesh and bones decapitate like soft butter. Only when nightfall comes that he turns into a human again. There are two ways to keep him from turning into a Vampire wolf, he should at least cover himself with a cloak from sunlight or get away from the same source of amount of light as the sun. And I will provide him with the black gem to contradict the UV rays."

The summer solstice of the same year has arrived in the northern hemispheres. Zenie at the age of fifteen has developed extra intelligence, height, and grown muscles. One morning, the boy discovered himself after rising up from his bed; Every inch of him is sore, he just realized that his open window are on the east side meaning he was exposed to the rising sun that literally burned his skin off, he was told by his father he would one day turn into something as he described himself just now...the first time he witnessed a such change in himself first than anyone else in the house. There was charred tissue on his bedsheets, and the smell was new to his sniff. He noticed his bed collapsed due to his extra weight. Startled from seeing what he doesn't understand, including the feeling of his extended muscular wolf arms and sharp claws, he started thinking... to go to their wood cabin. Afraid of himself being discovered and ostracized when town people might learn, he snuck up to his father's closet. But something unbelievable just occurred, he had felt the power of speed he wasn't accustomed to, in fact, had reached his dad's closet in the basement where he kept away long coats and cloaks for winter in a couple of seconds. He outbalanced himself but fortunately regained it when he braced himself with his claws. "They're beautiful and scary," leaving a certain long scorched mark on the wall down by the stair.

I slowly sneaked up out through the back door, gently with my fingertips, but when I heard mom get off her bed, the slightest sound made happened to get intensified and quite audible to my ears, unintentionally broke off the door's handle and fled to the wood cabin without notice from my parents.

"Sorry, mom for scratching your wall and breaking the doorknob. I am scared of myself and uncertain whether I could do more damage on my way anywhere."

There's nobody out there to guide me. But I only hear a low growl from my sadness and fear intertwined. Then my belly growled even louder, "I was hungry."

The excruciating pain was there. I bolted to go under the shade of trees but still, the stinging and the feeling of hot air coming out from all over me keeps me to bolt from one point to another.

I sensed two old people chatting from where I rested, and with thermal visions, I could tell their body heat signature had altered. They experience fear. Wolves from the forest roamed and three of them big and fierce and hungry sprung up. I rescued the couple from an animal attack.

Mr. and Mrs. Brown wondered how exactly they were saved and who did. Nobody saw how the three wolves disappeared so unbelievably quick, but there was a swift shadow paired with a streak of flaming red eyes.

"Maria, we are not harmed, the wolves have vanished before our eyes!"

Maria looked around, "where could they have gone?" She asked the husband...who thought only of one thing, the old story "they said... THERE'S A GUARDIAN IN THE FOREST that captures wolves."

The couple proceeded home and not far from where they had the vanishing wild attack, they met with the two guys, asking in a good manner if they could have some apples, although they admitted they'd no money. The nice couple gave them four and warned them to stay on the road. "Just warning, there are wolves around here that you probably might encounter...they don't hesitate to attack."

"Sir, you knew a log cottage around here?"

The old man replied with his concealed judging eyes, "yes... about a couple of miles from here, the woods are the shortcut though...you knew Dr. Joshu, he's the owner, are you going to rent it?"

With a quick response despite the lies, "we are not going to rent it, we are relatives of theirs."

"Does he know you are coming tonight?" The old man wanted to confirm.

The short guy although irritated with the query wanted to conclude the questioning, "yes we talked to Dr. Hoshu two days ago before coming here...thanks for the apple, ma'am...sir."

The wife was perceivably speechless, the husband notifying, "what's wrong, Maria?" She answered with precaution and gaze back to where the two guys went. "I recognized those two, they were posted everywhere in town, escaped prisoners on the run."

"I noticed our conversation, they're a bunch of imposters. First, they ask where the cottage is, Dr. Joshu always gives a map to anybody, relatives, or customers who may want to stay in, second...they admit Dr. Joshu knew they were coming, but he never mentioned this to me this morning. Third...they said they were relatives but couldn't even utter his last name correctly. The short guy said...Dr. Hoshu." The old man smirked.

The couple has decided, "we should inform the doctor, right away..."

For a few more hours, the exhausted Tom and Frank, persistently tracked the familiar scratches of claws after the two decided to fan out to quickly find clues of rapid trails of the wolves, that ended up in a nearby log cabin. They waited until the sun sets completely. A few more minutes and Tom ordered Frank to linger around the cabin, with assurance he reported back that there's only a boy napping on the couch. And Tom decidedly approved. "...it's time to break into the cottage."

Surprise...surprise, but Zenie's extraordinary sharp wit and cognizance outsmarted the two intruders.

After slamming the door inward, the unexpecting intruders were shocked by the boy's ready appearance, pointing a shotgun. The boy didn't flinch at all, he knew that would come, and the two known faces in his visions now appeared in front of him.

"You two were wanted and had thrived to escape." You two better leave...I am the *wrong guy* in your very *wrong place*...that's why I let my friends (the three wolves) go because I don't want them to get involved and get hurt, I knew something bad will happen tonight until tomorrow."

The one shorter holding a throwing knife threatened me with a bluff, "Hey kid, if you want to threaten us, make more effort...you haven't killed anyone yet, have you, boy? I can see from the shaking hand...you might probably haven't inspected your gun if it's loaded. I bet it's empty!"

I answered like a weird all-knowing person, "what if I'm just faking my trembling hands?" And creepily tilted my head like waiting for their reaction, the shaking stops, cocks the shotgun! Eyes squinted and upset!

And Frank, the shorty guy, started swinging to sling his knife upon hearing sarcasm.

My swift eyes saw the slight slow-mo swinging movement of shorty's hand and fired at the knife. Broken into pieces, the knife's shards scattered on the dusty floor. Plus, slightly injured shorty on his right hand. Blood and a bit of skin sprayed away in mid-air. I turned red instantly, but nobody notices.

"Owww!! That's stinging hurt, you son..."

"Don't you become aggressive on him; he's just scaredy-cat boy, just look what you ended up to." And he laughed, but while laughing, he swiftly distracted my thought and promptly aimed to grab the gun by its barrel direct to the far safe side and give me a right uppercut jab to my tummy. Knocked off, they tied me by a chair. All that time, I pretended, that the uppercut didn't cause me any pain nor knock me down; I knew my visions very well.

A few more minutes after regaining consciousness but uselessly tied up on a chair, I drew the angry short guy's attention and ended up giving me strong punches in the face! Man, my nose bleeds!

The taller guy munching his bread for night's snack interrupted. "Enough, how could we ask for the ransom if you'd already killed him?"

I heard my stomach growl. "I'm hungry. Can you feed me or give me some of your food?"

"You're not in the position to request something, boy, better starve, so you won't have the strength to escape."

"Yes, my father can give you what you want... (breathing sharply), but let's wait when my father comes in the morning."

Six in the morning, the sun's still not up. Someone's coming, a couple heading the way to the fence gate of the cabin.

The two 'wanted' burglars meet the couple outside. They brought cash in the pouch bag, but the couple wearing cloaks stops by ten meters from the porch.

"We are the parents of the boy...the life of the boy in exchange for a sum of your ransom money!"

Bad guys yelling from their distance, "How do we know you aren't armed?"

They showed their hands up in the air and demanded to release their son unharmed, and out of the house. "Then you can have your money enough to leave this town and have a new life in far-flung places. Do we have a deal?"

Almost sunrise. The boy's abductors have the shotgun and drag their bonded hostage, and as the request mentioned, the outwitted burglars exposed themselves outside but left the boy behind on the porch. The two forwarded, armed with shotgun and knife, to meet the couple. They walk cautiously towards the cloaked couple. He was about to shoot because the father won't give the money so easily unless they must release the boy, although Zendre was told beforehand by Elder Brother to buy more time until the sunlight reaches the porch; that's the PLAN!!!

Too gullible, they turned their back on the couple to grab the boy to untie him, in slow mo, the rope snapped and fell to the porch floor. It's too quick that normal eyes couldn't witness a very impressive speed. "Where's the boy?" He was right behind us!"

"Somebody has taken him!" *Yelled shorty. Nobody saw the boy has turned into a vampire wolf! The rushing speed of the beast smacked run over the two bad guys. All upper limbs were decapitated by the dashing strong swiping hand claws in his beast form.* ***With the power of the red gem to slow the time, and conjure an Enochian whisper, Elder Brother had seen it all.***

Its cutting motion resembles a Japanese sword cut. Swoosh away to hide the supernatural but stained stature. He halted. Gasping for an air of that speed behind bushes, he examined closely how strong his hand claws were.

The two brothers followed his track and the smell, surprised by the tall, frightening transformation, Zenie turned his broad, furry, slightly crouched shoulder and disclosed himself face to face with the couple. But to their ears are all growls and roars. "Who are you?" *Zenie asked them again,* "who are you?"

His profusing fiery aura, although not seen by the brothers, and due to his long weary night without food, he supported his weight with his weak shaking arms, his piercing eyes' no longer intimidating, and is about to shut...Zenie passed out!

Brother Narija saw nothing of the furry beast's appearance from a distance because of so many shadows around the cabin. But he's sure he saw the emblem on the back of their cloak glowed a bit but not too bright in response that there's a presence of anything from the three realms.

He thought of acknowledging himself for not bringing the other sword and wearing an average cloak. If ever, it would respond to glow in the dark, and he would be caught stalking.

The couple unveiled their cloak, and it was my father and Elder Brother, after all. Father's eyes were all tears, wanted so bad to hug his son! "This is so disturbing, knowing that you haven't eaten in a day and a half." Elder Brother cautioned my father by grasping his cloak by the shoulder to halt him.

The beast bowed his head until he fainted in front of them.

The father grabbed the broad furry body of his son and hugged him while he whimpered.

"What has happened to you?" Tears shed down his cheeks as he looks and seeks Elder Brother's guidance. Elder Brother knelt as his eyes explore; he took the big arm and hand focusing on the V-mark claws. Weighing his two hands together, he discerned it to be forty to fifty pounds. "My God... this is bloody heavy, a killing beast's claws!"

"He is not a pure evil vampire wolf, Zendre. He's still your boy, and even with that scary transformation, his mind is not affected; I've read an archive by our ancestors' brothers regarding vampire wolf's transformation. I believed Zenie is not the first.

Come on... he needed to be fed inside." Answered Elder Brother.

CHAPTER FOUR

A COVENANT

Despite my teenage hyperactive behavior and as the predator kingdom survivor, I have to fulfill my great plan. This is how I did. Right now, I am in the dungeon, no one knows but three members, and one of them is at the mercy of my wolf's hand claws. I'm strangling Brother Narija's neck against the cold rock wall of the mazy dungeon. It was my first time noticing that my claws have a V-shape mark on them, belonging to the vampire wolf species. Might not understand well how I turned into a vampire wolf in the dark, with the aid of the work of art of both my father and Elder Brother who designed a black crystal containing a manipulative spell of controlling my transformation wherever I go. It's inside the locket I wear around my neck. The sun is no longer a problem, the burning pain of transfiguration to a Vampire wolf is limited to an enduring capability. So, my transformation still depends on exposure to a strong bright light but with my necklace, it's controlled under my will.

With the help of the black locket, I can speak the human language in a harsh but low tone even in the vampire wolf transformation. I explained to curious Narija while pressing him against the rough stone wall. "The day in my transformation in the wood cabin, I was fully aware how many people were around me; Snarling and angry I expressed, "there were six, two burglars, the couple who saved me from being a hostage (Elder Brother and my father), and two hiding from bushes in the distance." He growls lowly and continued his revelation to Narija.

"The person hiding in the distance was you... and another farther one stalking behind you...someone you knew."

"You knew when the couple uncloaked themselves revealing their identities, which automatically revealed who I was in the scene because my father held me tight and whimpered. While you were behind that bush, your intention, whatever it is, is all yours because I also have mine. I already have told everything to the couple about my plan for you, but they also have planned something for me. Let us play my version, my plan against your plan. What do you say, Brother Narija?"

That was the next day when I snuck up into the Brotherhood's sanctuary, and I waited down the mazy dungeon, fitted for my plan, as I have instructed my father and Elder Brother to do what I exactly have in mind. That is for them to lure Brother Narija down into the dark dungeon because he kept following them and spying on all their moves. The careful instructions to them happened after I woke up as a normal human from my transformation in the wood cabin. I also have witnessed the first creepy encounter, when they put back all the decapitated limbs to those burglars without requiring medical instruments or stitches. They just allowed the burglars to drink the immortal water diluted with a tap, a formula written in the Book of the Three Realms to heal deep wounds or cuts but not to make them immortal. Only a pure liquid procures immortality.

The decapitated limbs were held to attach closely to the quick healing fresh-cut arms, and tissues like ligaments, bones, nerves, blood vessels, muscles, and skin bind like magic with no traces of scars left.

"If you want to investigate what I am talking about regarding the two burglars, they're both alive, with their limbs intact, back inside Victory prison."

All these came from Elder Brothers' knowledge as I observed him treat the two unconscious injured. I guessed he knew much stuff about the three realms, deadly, immortality, and predators.

Back to entrapping a witty spying brother, I showed my ferocious face as I breathed on Narija; he was terrified of my predatorial instinct that he thought I would munch out his face like a piece of prey meat. I could smell his fear at the time. Despite the fear, he asks me one question, after knowing that I could talk in whispers.

"Why are you saying this all to me?" Asked Brother Narija with his reading eyes stuck on the beast.

The beast snarls while continuously speaking to Narija. "So, I have my control over you. I don't care even if you're one of the twelve warriors, Narija. I don't care even if you dare to tell everything you saw to the Great Brothers of Congregation. Anyway, my visions are the final answer, and as for you, whether you are against me or not, is your choice.

"Now you saw everything, for now, you can live because it's your right, but by the time you speak up and reveal about us to the Great Congregation, I will not pose a threat to your life and to all your bloodline. Why? Because Vampire wolf does not threaten, I only hunt down to save the victims. So, hunting my target even in the dark isn't a big deal!"

His devouring eyes started blazing like red fire.

"Even you admit now you have no personal issues with either Dr. Zendre or Elder Brother, **I can still sniff the intention deep within your mind. In short, you cannot lie, you cannot hide.**"

The Great Congregation is situated in the western Mediterranean Sea. This island is self-sufficient to have trading civilizations, and in the middle of the land's summit occupies a fortressed-walled stronghold where ruling and governing dominion of the Brotherhood of the Eldest reside, in addition, they have educational services of Auran academy, school of Military and lastly the School of Deadly. All comprise the retired from their Brotherhood service who wish to continue to do three duties for the Brotherhood worldwide -to support, control, and ostracize, after obligated to conduct Wisdom Trial acting accordingly once summoned. Their aura manipulations aid them in supernatural transformation, strength, speed, and intelligence, including longevity.

"Now, let's come to an agreement, let's make it personal this time. I am Zenie, the only son of Dr. Zendre Joshu, who's a co-member of yours in the Brotherhood of Wisdom...of the Black Wolf region. If you point out Dr. Zendre Joshu and Elder Brother to the congregation, which cost them a lot of contingencies, tearing down their life and honor, I will unleash the two burglars from the prison and bring them to your family's home. This isn't a threat, it's a covenant between the two of us...because I don't see of this in my vision."

"Why not kill me, now...if you consider me as a threat or enemy?" Narija reasoned out.

"I don't kill my victim; I play with them...to know who stands out as PREDATOR in here." He raised his upturned middle claw pointing at his temple. "...until I find their mind not worthy opponent to play with under my underestimating test." And the Vampire wolf vanished leaving a black mist.

A week after that, one full moon evening on Sunday, there's like people in the town, gathering in every corner, watching and talking in whispers as they await the arrival of four carriages parading on the purpose of being summoned to the region's brotherhood. All four carriages have similar rounded infinity symbols of a serpent. My perception tells me they're the Great Brothers of Congregation, so I ask one public servant, an officer, for verification. It's a surprise. I was there too, I recalled what I just warned Brother Narija, but he's clean; he didn't report it.

Immediately I rushed to the Brotherhood of Wisdom. Because I know they hate surprises, and into the woods, I transformed into my beast form. Whenever I metamorphose, there's a sense of forcing warm air around me, and I feel heavy and strong. The transformation is the fast way to get to the Brotherhood and school of Alchemy and Wisdom. I am looking for any warrior brothers post up by their balconies from where I was running and closing in, but there's no sign of them. So that's where I got through. Disguised and dressed up like brothers, I was able to tell my father, and he alarmed the Elder Brother. Eventually, everyone got prepared even before the four carriages arrived.

Monday morning at the banquet hall...

Finally, the deliberation to conduct the Wisdom Trial by the Great Congregations of a series of investigations through cross-examination has been set to date. "...that will be tomorrow, ten in the evening sharp, Tuesday. As of your daily routine, nobody is restricted, your Brotherhood of Wisdom is under the administration and management of your highly assigned personnel with your Elder Brother taking full charge of it. That concludes this gathering...thank you, all brothers."

That night Elder Brother talked to Dr. Zendre about how the manners it's going to be held. He told him they are to find out if there is a presence of anything from the three Realms hiding on the mainland because they have brought with them the Realm god, and the god they are referring to can detect anything that came from or that belongs to the three realms.

"So, you are referring to my son."

"Yes, of course...it's like a monster can only detect another monster... because your son has the three components of all three realms- the blood of the Vampire Wolf, the immortality sap that he drank, and the deadly black quartz to manipulate his transformation. That realm god will arrive on the last day, but we must banish your son away from England before that would come. As in overseas. It's the only best solution we've got or else..."

"Or what?" Zendre began to worry.

"You and I who unofficially performed the realm endowment will be exiled and be sealed inside the realm door, and your boy will become the property of the greedy Congregation once found." Explained the Elder Brother.

My father and Elder Brother's plan, to banish me from the country, from my family, and from the Wisdom, has taken place the next night, Tuesday. My voyage to the East has been their next resort whenever Congregation's investigation would come up. I saw my mother, and it hurts her feeling.

I felt terrible seeing them like that, embracing tightly with each other while blaming themselves for their recklessness.

Just one thing that gave me a lesson, "**preparedness is at the top of any line of choices, including related coincidences, to avoid falling into messes.**"

While the ship bound to China is boarding travelers, I'm mourning as if it's my funeral.

"And as for the summoner, the one who reported to the brothers of the Congregation, I will deal with you later!" Having no knowledge of the fact, my hands, and fingernails elongated forming claws.

I'm thinking of the last stalker behind Brother Narija, the sixth person in the woods. The sadness on my face while deducing the past chapters was because I recalled my covenant with Brother Narija in the dark maze dungeon. He has nothing to do with the arrival of the Congregation and it's the last resort of the Congregation to summon on the last day the awakening of the Realm god, which leads to the exposure of evidence (myself). That the governance of Elder Brother may have come to its final demise. It's all my fault, my stupid curiosity.

"Will I grow up without seeing my mother and father? Is this really happening?" My tears are shrouding my sight, the drifting boat worsens it, even how hard I try to fold up my shirt to pat it. I bit my lip, but nothing compares to what I felt is stinging!

Later that night, on to the Wisdom Trial as the Great Brotherhood Congregation calls it, presided under Chief Andra's power and administration together with another Chief chaired by Chief Sophra, at random interrogation, Brother Zendre's turn has come up. The prosecutor who handled came from the in-charged: the School of the Deadly (secretly called the Aurans school of the Great Congregation) was called and presented the crimes of the accused: Brother Zendre Joshu and Elder Brother of the Brotherhood of the Black Wolf, and School of Alchemy and Wisdom are paying the ransom of the kidnapped, the victim involved is the fifteen-year-old son of Dr. Zendre Joshu who asked aid from Elder Brother to deliver the money, there was a gunshot and screaming and the emblem of the Black Wolf Brotherhood behind the cloak of the Brothers detected a presence of Realm entity as it was seen by a witness. A Brotherhood of any type disclosed to be hiding, harboring unofficial live creatures from the Realm kingdoms is illegal.

My father told his story, his tampered version goes like this, he did it on purpose as the blood is thicker than water goes: He and my mother had misunderstandings, yelling around the house was overheard by me, and my father reasoned their fight or misunderstanding as to my ground to fled away on my own, but he really knew where to find me.

"What misunderstanding was this, Brother Zendre?"

Father invented that mom and I disagree with his nightshift timetable in coming in to work to the Brotherhood. As I was on my way to our log cabin, my father narrated that he followed me, he saw two guys, an average height, and a short one, tracking down at me. My father expected them that they would follow me to the woods. As a matter of fact, he told the Congregation that his son can handle thugs and knows how to defend himself, using a shotgun. And so, he just left and came back the next day.

On his way back home, as he planned to bring a gun and ask Elder Brother's help, he saw a poster of wanted runaway, two faces of kidnapped for ransom prisoners who had escaped months ago since. He recognized their faces. Those were his son's intruders. That's when Dr. Joshu asked Elder Brother's help to deal with the intruders of his boy, turning bundles of paper into fake money.

"We reached the cottage; I saw my son as hostage, all tied up standing on the porch. His abductors were negotiating with us. But we're suddenly distracted by an ambush of several wolves; The one holding a shotgun was attacked first. The other hostage-takers yelled, "somebody has taken the boy!" We both heard a gunshot... scream, while Elder Brother and I crouched to the ground, as lower as possible, trembling with fear."

"Who took your boy away?" The interrogator cross-question.

"Pack of wolves, we had tracked him down because of his blood and ended up finding him unconscious."

"Final question Dr. Zendre Joushu. Why do you think they left your son?"

Brother Zendre recalled what happened to him with his son in the Predator's kingdom. "I believe it's their predatorial instinct to lure more preys to come over."

It's five after midnight. "Someone had seen you both from behind and we call them next for cross-examination. But the interrogation will happen tomorrow. So, we call it a night, all brothers."

"Thank you for your cooperation, Dr. Zendre Joshu." The Chief Congregation leader concluded and adjourned the trial that evening.

At the end of the first Wisdom Trial, Dr. Zendre had to meet Elder Brother in his office; although the Great Congregation had allowed them of their usual daily routine and practices, Dr. Zendre noticed that Elder Brother had minimized chatting with everyone regarding the happening.

Dr. Zendre has come to see his friend Elder Brother, while he has the chance, that whatever consequences would arise the next day from the next person, he'd just want to thank Elder Brother for giving him a hand despite his short time of service in the brotherhood.

"I can never forget you, my brother friend; because of you, I know my entire family is safe. I have no regrets about whatever I have mentioned (lies) earlier. You know I must. The Brotherhood needs you and not me."

"Ssshh...they can hear you, and you know I couldn't seal this room. *They* might suspect us. But you amazed me."

There was a slight misunderstanding that Dr. Zendre couldn't follow, and he wrinkled his brows. Elder Brother resumed his explanation.

"Those members of the Great Congregation are a bunch of *readers*, and so, do I, but I *read* them too, and I found no doubts or suspicion was playing in their mind against your deliberation. I'm guessing you can conceal your thoughts; it's your gift after drinking some immortality liquid. *I'm right with my hypothesis all along* that immortality has something to do with concealing-mind ability functions."

After midnight that same night, no one noticed a quick-moving entity had gotten through the Brotherhood's domain through the upper balcony. A mysterious hooded man appears after dissipating his darkest aura.

CLIFF GAP
BLACK WOLF BROTHERHOOD
OPENING LEADING TO TUNNEL
TUNNEL
CHAMBER OF GATEWAY
CROSS THE GATEWAY
PREDATORS KINGDOM

CHAPTER FIVE

THE HUNTING GROUND VIEW

There was a shadow of a hooded figure and creep up to all three doors that belonged to the quarters of Dr. Zendre, Elder Brother, and Brother Narija respectively, but the hooded figure pressed his hand to leave a sweat mark, not just a normal sweat mark, it's under something to control.

Around three A.M., Wednesday...

Three big black wolves came running down the rock mountain, while crossing the heart of the woods, one of them slowed down and took a glance at something sniffed, the beast had found something from the ground, pick it up, and proceeded back with the two beasts and have arrived in the School of Alchemy and Wisdom.

One of them is carrying a leader bag collared around its neck, the leather bag, and its content is for Elder Brother, a letter, and a fragment of the knife.

Routing through the lower balcony only one has entered, where it was intendedly left open by the tall shadow hooded figure. That black wolf moved toward where it respectively sniffed the sweat mark using its sight of hunting ground that can distinguish to follow where it leads...to the door of Elder Brother. The huge black wolf looked fixedly at Elder Brother. And by their exchange of looks, the black wolf delivers mind whispers, messaging Elder Brother that they were ordered to pick him up, including Brother Zendre and Brother Narija.

"By whose authority?" Asked Elder Brother as he gets near to give the creature a nudge on its head. The creature whispered an indistinct answer. There's a letter for him, from the mysterious hooded man.

To Elder Brother,

Never mind who wrote this letter, it's urgent to win your case against the Great Congregation, and whoever will emerge as a witness in the end, but I have already seen the vivid consequences of the trial.

The three Black Wolves will be yours, and they will answer to your Auran orders anytime you want them as additional to your twelve Wolf Warriors, symbolizing your Brotherhood, complete with a collar made of a metal I only have procured, copying your Black Wolf emblem. The metal is made originally in your world, not in my world, but with the contamination of my DNA, the reaction has turned the metal into a useful, anti-detection of the glowing cloak of all Brothers, Warriors, and even the Deadly (the Aurans).

Consider me as your friendly Guardian or a friendly god allied to your Brotherhood of the Black Wolves of the England region; inside the leather are pieces of nails made in my world but from the metal, I mentioned earlier that came from the reaction of my DNA. Use this to build a podium, where weight of a hundred and fifty pounds to three hundred pounds man can withstand and place it in the center where the witness will be called.

The back of this letter is a map leading the three of you into the gateway, that rested in a chamber since the dawn of the first settlers, the Glowing Deadly. Once you reach the Chamber of the Gateway, the presence of the three black wolves will allow the opening of the gate belonging to the creatures, and you will enter my Predators' kingdom. Go, ride with the Black Wolves and they will lead you to me, here in the Howling Wolf Mountain, now.

Your Ally,

The Mystery Hooded Man.

Elder Brother smiled after sensing a relief. Despite the weird and absurd encounter, he called both my father and Brother Narija, after knowing there was a sweat mark of humanoid wolf pressed on his door too, using his luminaire eyes. The summoned brothers came up to the agreement to come along. The three Brothers have noticed the giant wolves have a round, and flat tag collar dangling with the emblem of the Brotherhood. The giant creatures are new to Elder Brother but under the command of the mysterious hooded figure who wanted to meet the three Brothers. Only Elder Brother knew he did recall that he gave one to me, the same symbol of midnight Canis lupus itched.

Elder Brother explained to them both what he had read...that they have a chance to win the Wisdom Trial...by the help of one Mysterious Hooded Man.

"Listen, you two, but whatever we are going to find out..."

"Find out where?" Questioned Dr. Zendre to the interrupted Elder Brother.

Elder Brother continued, "I have read the summoner's messages of this beast to meet up with him?"

"Who's him, Elder Brother?" Both asked.

"A predator god," Elder Brother made that up. "And I want to see, because according to the summoning god, a door has been opened, and we are his guests inviting us to go over there." Explained Elder Brother whispering his voice.

"Where is there...Elder Brother?" Asked Brother Narija.

"We have to see for ourselves, come on." Persuaded Elder Brother to the two.

Riding on the three big black wolves heading towards the hill after the forest, they come to set on their feet to get closer. A not so steeply hill collapsed to make an opening deep down a dirt tunnel, marvelously made by a force. They walked with caution that was led by Elder Brother requiring his deadly magic expertise. With his touch on the dirt wall, he ignited all the hidden crystal gems embedded. From the looks, it was an ancient tunnel during the early civilization of the Deadly (the Aurans) and is protected under the auran spell and even buried for countless centuries. And they see a dead end, but a wider round chamber of an ancient structure crafted out by early unmanned tools. Up ahead aligned to the opening is focal that heeds their attention, a huge triad of structure protruding from the opposite wall and it began to move towards them mysteriously but hovering up to the center. Although covered with aged roots hanging and clinging, the roots burned into dispersing red ashes, and the whole floating structure emerged to their wonder. They noticed their *Black Wolf emblem* from the back of their cloak started glistening. From where? They turned and with their marveling mind, the beasts' three necklaces are giving off light, hindering the flow of energy to the outside surface of the human world.

After getting into the gateway, the entire hovering structure dissipated its glow and attached itself back to the wall of the big round chamber.

Upon crossing the realm door riding with their wolves, the familiar smell rings a bell to my father, "can we slow down a little?" He's nauseated and started vomiting.

As they all passed by the two gigantic obelisks with wolves grotesquely carved figures each on top, "You are too frightened, brother Zendre. We are invited as guests in this kingdom, not as dinner."

Still unaware of who summoned them, the three Brothers of Wisdom finally arrived at the wolf's territory called the Mountain of the Howling Wolf through the large brick slabs path guided by pairs of burning gem torches along the road, leading to the highest peak in entire kingdoms. They rode through the rocky made underground with columns of calcified rocks sculptured by auran powers of manipulation holding the ceiling that showed blown-mind marvels to their eyes as they travel along. The inside of the more spacious vicinity had shown proof that advance minded race of occupants had lived there for centuries.

"A great city perhaps a kingdom during their time inside a mountain?" The astounded Elder Brother detailed.

Looking around, Brother Narija pondered, "Yes a city indeed, but where is everybody?"

"Everything begins and ends, nothing provides immortality, just longevity, brothers."

They walked down the irregular stair, but its arch below is supported by used abandoned mechanized mega tools that collaborate to its stability, no one knows if they're still operational.

Crossing the large bridge structured inside a hollowed mountain, my father cannot believe how all those precisions have accomplished such advanced wonders, "What kind of technologies are applied here?"

Elder Brother smiled as he answered his question, "the Deadly Aura... what else?" And into the vast cave of Howling Wolf Mountain, three gates have been observed by the three Brothers, a gate before the bridge, another gate entering the city, and finally a gate that would open in the presence of the three Black Wolves, never to be opened manually because that's impossible as they all saw how wide and thick the carved rock gates are made of.

So, the final gate opens to the semi-circular wall like in a huge stadium. And in the middle is a wide-like arena, where bonfire crystal lights up and warms the freezing cavern, where wolves are scattered around. By the side of it flows a natural cave river on a shallow gully where it leads to another cave opening.

While the three beasts lowered their riders in front of the unidentified summoner, they set foot with wonders as to who the summoner might be. Weapons and their cloak glowed in response to the presence of three realm creatures, the tall, hooded figure appeared, and the wolves all bowed down. Seeing with their luminaire eyes the tremendous fiery gold flaming auras the tall, hooded figure emanates, he slowly unveiled his cloak. It's a Vampire wolf in the humanoid form...transformed into a normal fifteen-year-old kid.

"My god!! It's Zenie?" Elder Brother stated in confusion.

"How did you end up here?" The father interrogates.

"It was me, the summoner, the mysterious hooded man, the god predator."

Elder Brother has acknowledged something's changed from Zenie. He now can transform into a Vampire wolf even without the aid of the black locket. The wolf came nearer to Zenie and bowed to bring back to him another piece of the second fragment of the knife.

"Elder Brother, you have noticed that I need not worry to wear the will transformation locket in my kingdom but in the human world I will still wear it, or I will burn. It was me who wrote you..."

"Father, Elder Brother, and Brother Narija, Welcome to *the* Underground Wolf *chamber*, also known as the Howling Wolf Mountain. Do not worry...nobody can stalk us here, and before that could happen,

I first could catch them out!" He flaunted a vanishing act after ragingly emanating a black aura, darker than any shadow. And came back behind them while the three were still facing the direction he had charged on.

"I didn't pursue on voyaging to the East, not now...because my actual time and existence as god predator here have just begun!"

He looked at Brother Narija and walk side by side heading out, and the father interrupted, "what do you mean, son, by time and existence of yours, has begun?"

"As god predator?" Elder Brother whispered, really acknowledging that Zenie had transcended.

The young boy looks back at his father, "I'll explain to you later, father."

Zenie explained to brother Narija while strolling outside the cave into the dark woods. Narija felt the fear of being alone with a supernatural Zenie and the fear of walking into the midst of the pitch-black darkness of a natural forest...realizing that he can transform into that intimidating and frightening creature.

"Don't be frightened, I will just open up something for your understanding...**because understanding is power, contrary to arrogance as powerless!"**

"I call it the Hunting Ground view," the boy introduced and resumed his explanation when Brother Narija shows his interest.

"You know most cases, everyone's afraid in the dark...because they lack the senses to move into the dark. For me, I will wait for my eyes to adapt, then I can move."

"That's how these nocturnal creatures utilize the hunting ground view at night. Their sights, including mine, can scour everything at any time here like during daytime. **In your darkness, I can defeat you**."

He asks brother Narija to allow his left fingertips to meet his right fingertips. Zenie's nails transformed into the beast's protruding vampire wolf's claws, sharp and pointy that pierced each of Narija's fingertips. It stings! The idea he told Narija to see for himself the experience of the Hunting Ground view. But when he asks brother Narija to turn back, there was an enlightened spirit, his body is glowing. The rocky cave mountain from the outside resembles the landscape of a howling wolf. Full of glowing auras from creatures of the pack of wolves. Beautiful than the Aurora Borealis in the northern sky.

"It's beautiful as the beasts of this territory look up to it the way you respect it now with such astound feeling, but before... you never notice anything. Like those average hikers and hunters, very shameful that they don't see any existence of the World, ravaging anything using their futile senses of darkness, that's why even their understanding is shrouded with forever darkness, the arrogance of imbecilic comfort."

"Why are you doing this to me, Zenie?"

"Because I've simply given you a line of defense... for tomorrow's cross-examination and interrogation..."

"Now fight me, Brother Narija, use your realm sword!"

"I won't fight you. You're not intimidating as I can perceive!"

"But I see your sword is responding that a three-realm creature is in front of you...How about now?"

I have emanated flaming golden auras, more immense than before. It has consolidated into a giant ferocious humanoid vampire wolf, double my height. Brother Narija flinched and stepped backward, knowing only a kid is in front of him, that's because Narija can now see my real energy of aura and what he really is with the imparted hunting ground sight.

"What you see now is my manipulated *auran image.* Never hesitate now that you understand what's in front of you, you will do the same tactic tomorrow, Narija. I am ordering you not as a child but as an apex predator. Swing your sharp sword!"

The striking with the sword can defeat a realm creature, but with an agile mind that he cannot only read but can divert and manipulate, Zenie didn't block his swinging sword, he dodges it and scratches it with his transformed sharp claws.

"Please, read my mind, knowing your opponent can tell you best what to utilize against him." My aura outpoured profoundly, and my red eyes glistened vividly.

Narija pierce a boulder from his side a three feet diameter and tossed it against Zenie. But Zenie didn't dodge it this time, he simply chops it with one swing, but Narija is already up above him ready to end the fight with a surprise big slash. The remaining golden flaming auras of the big vampire wolf were slashed diagonally and dispersed. The real Zenie has vanished in a flash looking at Narija from behind. Not only that, Narija has never noticed that Zenie has taken from the warrior his sword and impaled it deep to the ground kneeling.

"That was a good fight." I never told Brother Narija, that it was my doing how our fight goes to end. I faked my applause to cheer Narija. I promised I wouldn't leave them unprotected...and till they're ready.

"Brother Narija Martin, I want you to know this...someone you knew before will betray you." And they left the dark woods heading back to the underground wolf chamber.

The four of them sat around the crystal bonfire.

"The Great Brothers of Congregation has climbed up...flourishing to a covetous level of acquisition. Their power to reign over all Brotherhoods of Wisdom across the continent became blemished with political subjugation. However, meek presentation at the introduction, but their climax ends with fraudulence to trap anyone gullible enough to submit to their controlling grip."

"How do you know all this, young boy?" Asked the confused Elder Brother.

"I speak not as a child of my father, as you can see around us, I have something in me that this pack yields to my existence. The Congregation wouldn't leave England's Brotherhood empty-handed. Whether you like it or not, even you can get through the Wisdom Trial, they will do even the dirtiest to make things *even* with their opponent."

"Do you have any idea what you are saying may lead to?" The father asked.

"Yes...they want all the power, either good or ravaging, to be under their control...to wage a conquering war who are against them, and I am one... who is against them." Strongly stated Zenie with his voice as god predator. The scene of the discussion about the Wisdom Trial around the flaming gem bonfire faded to its illumination, but the conversation didn't stop there. It further resumed to another subject matter, the power of the Fourth Realm.

Wednesday night at ten P.M.

It's the night Brother Narija stood up to enlighten everyone on his concept in the trial court.

"I who belonged to the Brotherhood of Black Wolf, and to the School of Alchemy and Wisdom, never saw a beast, but that doesn't guarantee that there was no presence of beast lurking around, because I heard screaming about who'd taken the boy, and later I heard crying, a cry from a father to his injured son.

"There was a story that the two hostage-takers were killed by the beast, wasn't there?" Asked one interrogator.

"Killed? Sorry for the laugh, that I find it amusing, really! Who told you such sloppy fabrication?" So responded Narija doing the same as the readers are currently doing. Narija can read everyone's auras and even the kind of attitude attached to it to each one. He remembers how Zenie instructed him to read glowing auras, "intimidate the most glow of auras by looking at him in the eyes. They don't know or have no idea that you can read; they'll just slip it away and theorize."

While still looking at the most glowed aura among great Brothers that Chief Andra, he elaborated the rumored dead wanted jailbreakers with sturdy pride. "The two escaped prisoners had been inflicted with bruises and fracture, yes, due to sudden bashing from the speeding creatures, and had been traumatized by the unexpected, horrifying encounter. When everyone is under control, Elder Brother with his vested power of the learned Deadly, healed the fractured of the two thugs, emanating a strong Deadly aura that had caused the detecting cloak to glow in the dark woods."

"Right now, they were put back behind bars and are safely secured yet recovering. Conscious yet undeniably, they're unconditional to state any facts. I just had my personal visit to feed up my curiosity and interested motives."

Brother Narija explained to persuade his side of wisdom to all listeners and interrogators by drawing a scenario. Although slightly sarcasm shows in his eyes, he clears his throat.

"One lad, two burglars, and a couple of our brothers encountered an intelligent giant supernatural beast in the woods. Would you think the five of them could have survived such a horrifying experience and fled away from it without injury, scratch, decapitations, or even worse, death? I doubt it, fellow great Brothers of Congregation!"

"And would you think I could run faster and never been sniffed by the beast after stalking in the dark? To clarify everyone, I eat the most when it comes to spices among us!" Brother Narija added.

Chief Sophra asked. "Did you say you were stalking them?" Another question is thrown.

Brother Narija responded. "We have the rule in the Brotherhood...but like black wolves, we are pack. Everyone must commit to applying it at all costs, especially in times of danger; you know that our organization deals with either supernatural good or evil: AM I MY BROTHERS' KEEPER? My answer to that is a solid yes. **An injury to a fingertip may make or become an injury to the whole body!**"

"When I found out nothing suspicious was executed against the Brotherhood of Wisdom, especially on your behalf honorable Great Brothers, I left, and I thought twice no brother interrupts family matter unless they summon for help. I have recalculated and in the presence of the respected Elder Brother, the two of them can dwindle the scene of both escaped prisons causing public menaces and the wild beasts' attack."

And the great act begins. "Nothing of these might work as a reason to summon great Congregation, but we are honored for your concerned visit and stay with us. I've no idea, and to tell you... I feel jealous that Brother Zendre's family matter like the kidnapping and ransom trading in exchange for his son's life could summon our Great Brothers' generosities from overseas."

CHAPTER SIX

THE LAST WITNESS

This is Narija Martin, also called Brother Narija. Joined the Wisdom Midnight Canis lupus region in England for twenty years. I've never known all this time at the age of forty since it's been too long. That I've been pursued not by a stranger but by an old friend and an orphanage childhood.

It had started when I promised him a long time before we even get to part ways from the orphanage that I would impart something for him when my wish was granted to obtain supernatural power. We dreamed of wild imaginations of having some kind of magic good or evil, that is when we joined organizations of high societies of combined science and magic, the alchemists.

In short, as an orphan, I was introduced to the alchemist as a housekeeper, but that hard task, although very hard to some, my body and intellect wouldn't resist any job they demand. For them, I am a supernatural person that even sickness in the House of Wisdom won't affect me. Unaware that I had developed my immunities, many antibodies kept me protected from their illness and soon I became the doctor's helper. In the end, I earned their admiration until I became one of the brothers.

Known to the Brotherhood, I only have courage as power and the primary and straightforward magic of Luminaire eyes, until I met Zenie, the Vampire Wolf, whom I swore to keep (him) in secret. He's the only survivor of the realm of the Predator's Kingdom in the century, whom only four people in England knew of this secret, his mother, his father, Elder Brother, and me.

That promise isn't actually broken, but my orphan friend theorized that I have forgotten everything, the promise, the friendship, and him. And it turns out he's more on to his revenge on me for his greed and ambition to obtain power. I know him a lot; I grew up with him like an actual sibling, orphan children always recount him as power without control. I even sometimes get into trouble, sent to the directress' office, due to pacifying some fights that involved him.

"Yes, I remember him, the power without control; the power without the rule in body, mind, and soul would only be a danger creating much more trouble. So much worse when he accrued torment, he is worse than broken."

And that wisdom, I just had proven it just now. As their last witness, he was summoned by the Great Brothers of the Congregation to appear in the Wisdom Trial.

He uses his grudge against me to dishonor us by telling and reporting everything to the Congregation, even more, powerful than his courage knowing that one from the Congregation became his advocator. And his supporter made him into a spy and messenger ever since he took a chance of persistence of introducing himself one afternoon to one Congregation member by the gate when one carriage stops waiting for the gatekeeper. Fortunately, it opened up a good conversation knowing that they can use only one person. His name is Alexis. Alexis Fortuni.

"Who's bothering?" Asked an old bad-tempered Chief Brother of Great Congregation inside his carriage. He is usually the Chief of Courage, the authority of the Military and all defense in the great Congregation, but after Chief Ara of Virtue passed away, Chief Andra relieved the position.

"I am the witness, to stand on trial, not a member of the Brotherhood, but I knew what I saw that night after stalking one of the brothers that I used to know," Alexis replied straightforwardly.

"Let him in!" Ordered at once to his coachman.

Inside, Chief Andra in a thick black cloak lifted his chin and looked at him in the eyes. The brother froze, definitely scouring the mind of the stranger. And Alexis saw the hesitating Chief Brother smirked a little. Chief Andra who's grumpy and tired from his journey saw the courage in him. Apprentices wearing the dark-red cloak are Deadly readers, mind controllers, hypnotizers, or mental telepathists.

Alexis felt the coachee had U-turn the entire carriage instead of getting in through the gate. The apprentice did what was ordered on her, to mind control the coachman to bring them back to the town proper.

"Yes, I recognize you.... you're the reason why we're here in England.

Sitting beside the Chief Brother is another female apprentice, who wears the same dark red cloak of the Deadly, manifesting power of controlling the mind of what Chief Andra wanted the stranger to see, but not the actual dirty caressing of the body of her pretty apprentice.

The old grumpy Chief Andra and Alexis went to the nearby, ordering the coachee to linger around town. They talked about Alexis thought what really had transpired in the woods that night. After learning the truth that Alexis couldn't prove if it was supernatural or not, he begged he wanted revenge against his old friend (Brother Narija) who had promised him power; that's why he's doing all that to humiliate his old friend.

"How farther can you go, my friend?" Chief Andra reading his mind, asked him.

"You can use me, and I will take all the cost, as long as I can accomplish my revenge," replied Alexis with a smirk, evil intent.

"Okay, I make a deal with you...but make sure you do what I will instruct you. Lie and act to everyone that you saw a real beast taller than a human and that you saw their real cloak from your distance that it had glowed on their back, which shows a single proof that there was a presence of a realm creature that night you were creeping up on."

"But Sir, all your Brothers in the Congregation would know who's lying or not. I've heard Brothers of the Congregation region can elucidate things through reading mind, heart, and soul," worries Alexis.

"That's up to my apprentices." He looked at the one beside him, "she wouldn't let my Brothers read your mind, heart, and soul...only then that after the trial, I will give you what you asked for, but it could owe you much price."

Eleven o'clock sharp in the same evening, the trial resumed. Finally, they call upon the next witness, and as he marches into the center, silence filled the room due to the dramatic entrance of a hooded man walking, but as he was guided by the apprentice, the woman in a dark-red cloak, Alexis was entirely unidentified, entering while facing down the floor, left by the apprentice in the middle.

He unveiled himself, lowering his cloak exposing his identity as he turned around slowly to every gentleman's sight, smirking.

Brother Narija couldn't imagine how true Zenie's words were...

"Someone you know before will betray you soon." Brother Narija recalled.

After introducing the last stalker and the last witness, several questions were asked, almost the same as Brother Narija.

"You saw a beast that transformed from a normal human, is that account you just stated, right?"

"Yes."

"And who would that beast be? Have you identified the person?"

"It was dark, but I know it was from a human. There was something an average man like me can feel it's from a different world because...there was some energy forcing out from his body, and there was the speed in the activity."

"An auran...an auran..." Murmured the Brothers of Congregation.

"What's an au..auran, Sir?" Alexis stated a query.

"Any creature possessing supernatural power uses this full capacity of the brain, making or manipulating the energy of the body as a mere weapon or medium to execute an efficient and quick task of combat or healing. These energies can be in the form of light, shield, antigravity, transporting, strength, senses, drawing energy from, and more to discover."

A Brother from the Congregation stood... "In science, your body can function so many tasks externally and internally, imagine if you can order your brain to do a musculoskeletal job that is far more breakthrough compared to an average human simple task like lifting."

Alexis recognized where the voice came from; it was from his grumpy backup, Chief Andra.

"Final question, if you said there was a transformed human into a supernatural beast, why did all the witnesses closer to the beast left them unharmed?"

"Only a bloodline could unharmed his own family and friends." Face bowed down and slowly expressed his egoistic chin up while uttering his statement, an analytical response of the last witness Alexis. Brother Narija, Brother Zendre Joshu, and Elder Brother are astonished they didn't anticipate what the witness just stated.

Brothers from the side of the Congregation murmured and continued their low indistinct voices. Then, finally, some nodded to depict the last witness has some points. Tension has culminated in the hall, a lot of auras radiated, and Brother Narija can perceive such commotion and lavish aura manipulation where the Brothers of Congregation were under the blocked reading the mind and soul manipulation.

A few seconds before twelve midnight. With all the answers, Elder Brother fisted his two hands, wanting to stand and defend his Brothers on his side...but a sudden and actual confusion had occurred that no one among them expected. From the color-tainted glass windows, three big black wolves jump through and shatter them. Yet, dark as they get into the room, nobody recognized the three until their sharp eyes glowed as they growl, snarled, and ran straight to Alexis in the middle.

One first big black wolf snouted-thrust Alexis by the belly which launch him in momentum, the second big black wolf jumped high to clinch him by the waist, and the third black wolf tries to pull the witness' arm, but Elder Brother stood at once, "Stoppp, you are what you eat...that isn't a real meal, it's malady!!"

"I apologized for their entrance, I guess they can't wait to be summoned. When they sniffed a stranger and a fraud, they attack the first liar. The fact that these three Black warriors can not be controlled by any Deadly users." Explained Elder Brother.

"What's going on here? What are these black wolves doing in the Wisdom Trial?" The annoyed eldest Chief leader Andra of the Congregation brother stood. The interrogator, knowing the congregation, brought with them an intervening army of the black-red cloaked auran manipulators, ordered to get rid of the animals.

The two other wolves jumped as close as possible to the interrogator, who decided to sit down and shut up. Anticipating the consequences that the army of auran manipulators can handle the disturbance, started to perform an auran image, but it turned out the big wolves started to play with them and licked the army in their faces.

Elder Brother stood up and walked to the center controlling his smile. With pride and dignity...he answers the question of the interrogator.

"They are my **bloodline**...the work of my wisdom, as you can see all our cloaks' emblem shines, even our weapons' markings glistens. I found them when they were pups. But they aren't from the realm kingdom, because I took care of these pets when their mother took a fight with a grizzly and died. I turned them into better and more useful creatures, giving them the magic and science of alchemy. As you see them, they like to play and it's their gesture to show welcome to our guests.

With rage and strengthened spirit, he raised his voice. **"They are the *last witnesses* and not your lying scumbag witness...hoping on having himself an illegal power in exchange for all his fabricated lies."** Elder Brother put them back their collar tag and the auran detection cloak dissipated its glow.

"Nonsense! We don't see anything lies in all the testimonies of this man!" The defending advocator of Alexis objected.

"We don't see that because one is not present in the trial court. Bring back the woman in the black red cloak, and you will see." Elder Brother walks with the black wolves and continues elucidating the Congregation.

"He who doesn't appear in the court as a member among readers can seal and obliterate all fraud information, he or she can blind all senses from knowing the truth in his mind, heart, and soul." Explained the defensive Elder Brother.

"How do you know all these facts?" Chief Sophra, leader of the counseling and investigation, questioned him. "Don't tell me you have broken the rule to enter the forbidden archives?" Murmurs and indistinct inferences filled the entire hall while the Chief leader ordered anyone from making any noises clamors.

"Nothing in my domain has I broken, fully aware not to enter the forbidden archives or partake from anything of it. Everything in my head was endowed to me by my grandfather when I was a young boy, not even knowing my grandfather's position or rank in his region of Brotherhood."

The old man (Elder Brother) held his stand pointing and trembling at the executive table, **"...now, if you want to punish and detain my grandfather...dig his graveyard!"** As he welcomes them with open arms, and a slight smile.

Elder Brother bravely resumes his wisdom about managing his Brotherhood while facing everyone, and where he goes the three last witnesses (the Black wolves) walk beside him. "Knowledge or wisdom taken by breaking into the god-forbidden archives is punishable. **The archives control the person's mind in surmounting scale, rather than a person controlling his mind,** thus putting all Brothers in danger and death."

"But the wisdom imparted by someone isn't a crime. It's the instructing the implication of warning, to know the difference between experiencing and theorizing."

"My grandfather had experience with realm endowment. Unlike me, I have learned from him all the existing world of the endowment. He forbids me to enter even though the book says it's tolerable, and it's voluntarily, but in my strict control...I wouldn't tolerate it unless I have the perfect creatures to defend my Brothers from someone coming back the entry. Twelve Wolf Brother warriors aren't strong to guard or barricade if a Vampire wolf or Deadly magic creature crosses the realm door. That's why I have my pets."

"Now...bring back to the courtroom the woman in a black-red cloak." After demanding the Congregation, Elder Brother turned his back and proceeded to his seat, whispering to himself... **"I love to say I told you so with sarcastic rage... in your face!"** Smirked and shook his head slightly.

"Before the trial for tonight has been adjourned, there was a surprise. If the two prisoners cannot be invited due to their traumatic experiences, on behalf of Chief Sophra of the Investigation and Counseling, we would inform the validation of this Wisdom Trial will proceed until tomorrow when the last witness arrives." The presider spoke.

Thursday, ten AM, the last witness is called, there was no aura manifesting in the last witness as he marches down the hall, cloaked and hooded to be disclosed when called for interrogation.

When the witness revealed himself, it is Zenie.

"State your name, young man."

"Zenie Yeng Joshu."

"Do you believe in the Guardian of the woods?"

"Some of my schoolmates do, not me...but I know of wilds in the woods that serve the purpose of guards of the woods."

"When you disappeared, one of your abductors shouted hysterically that you were gone...how did you disappear from your spot?"

"If you want to run through the scene, that I cannot remember, I will ask you to tie a rope several rounds on me...then we'll see what's going to happen." Elder Brother smirked with delight.

"But you were found behind a tree without the rope."

"Yes, unconsciously."

"How did you get there, can you remember?"

"Whoever put me there behind a tree, must know the answer to your question, but the unconscious can never answer that even how many times you rephrase your query."

"You said whoever. What do you have in mind?"

"Whoever, whatever, whichever, whenever, wherever implies unknown or unspecified unless you were there consciously watching me."

A piece of paper of request is given to the interrogator, fold it to close, and asks two assistants to help him unclothe Zenie, leaving only his undergarment.

I don't know how my father would react to the request, including Brother Narija, both yelling in disgust and some others. "Zenie is the victim here, NOT the culprit, bloody moron!!!" Elder Brother consoled his brothers who are definitely irritated and infuriated by the acts done to a victim kid. Chief Andra demanded to resume the undressing. And they even order the kid to take off the locket (the DNA-contaminated metal knife casing a philosopher's stone). What was left is his underwear.

After a full minute, and a few seconds...Zenie spoke.

"Nothing happens, you came all the way here from a very long tiring journey believing a fraud envious troublemaker, now where did it get you?

Nothing. He has fooled you and cannot prove that I, a family member can turn into a monster and never harm the Brothers. Where is your wisdom yet you call yourself Congregation of the Wise Elders?

"Bless the Black Wolf Brotherhood, where the true PREDATORS of wisdom live on!"

The boy smiles in victory, including Elder Brother who did to finish the assigned wide elevated podium which uses the nails made from Zenie's DNA-contaminated knife metal. And from Zenies smile, it panned down to the podium.

CHAPTER SEVEN

THE CRIES OF MY PEOPLE

Gloomy Friday and about to drizzle, the expected day of the arrival of the Serpent god, prophesied through the grim vision of Zenie. The congregation has never proved of anything to demolish the Black Wolf Brotherhood but had left behind a Serpent god to find believed evidence of a lurking Wolf god covertly protected by the Wolf Brotherhood.

That same day, a brave boy like the age and height of Zenie, went to the woods to collect firewood. But what was unusual to that boy was that he is all messy with dirt, not mud, as if he excavated a deep pit. He is a young boy named Haniel, and when the scene panned where he came from tracing back his origin via his mud-spattered footprint, started from a mound graveyard freshly opened, besides it is a rock that had inscription unknown to human, but at the present moment that rock was all covered mossy and accumulated dirt through the ages. When Thaniel, the twin brother had succeeded to possess my body after negotiation in the Fourth Realm, his twin brother Haniel who harbors centuries of slumbering souls resurrects from his grave.

"I have never let you do things on your own, twin sons...because I can read your mind from a far distance, and my absence physically never ever meant abandoning you... ***and if only when things you can't handle arises...that's when I'm there to rumble!"***

-Father Idjiel of the Twin Brothers

Haniel continued picking up dried twigs, tripped himself, and fell into a ditch, all the collected got scattered, and his right hand got soaked into the mud; unaware when he lifted himself from the mess, his hand from the muddy ground got caught onto something, a chain with rounded flat object dangling. Wiped it with his shirt and saw an emblem, the god predator.

Walking home with it and some gathered firewoods made his day more satisfying than those usual days. Unknowingly he has walked outside the ranging shield of the gateway where the locket must not supposed to be exposed. It has gotten out far from the range of protective shield from its center, the ancient realm gate (to where the Three Brothers go through). And the farther the black gem in the locket was moved from the ranging shield source, (the Ancient Gadi Trinity emblem), it would draw attention to any Deadly manipulator (Auran).

Speaking of my locket, during my fifteenth birthday, a few months after, I started metamorphosing into a Vampire wolf, on earth, the UV rays of the sun would burn my skin, and becomes a Vampire wolf, without the curing aid of the Immortal sap in the system, I would burn to death.

My father and Elder Brother through thorough research using the sample blood and tissue, the two Brothers have come up to resolve the problem which has procured them the locket with a tiny fragment of the Black Monolith. With it worn, I could go around anywhere day and night, shielding me from the UV light or any bright light to turn into a Vampire wolf, in addition, it enhances my aura manipulation to control my will, which ensued I can turn with the command of my will and can go through the gateway to another World. The disadvantage, wearing the ordinary locket can draw much attention from Deadly users, accidentally I solved that dilemma to inhibit the Deadly users from perceiving one like me, my new locket case is made of a metal knife contaminated with the reaction of my DNA. The new metal casing of the locket can control or shield the Black Monolith and can shield the god aura who bears it, thus, with the new locket no Deadly user can identify me as somebody from the Realm on earth.

Back Tuesday at ten in the evening, when I boarded the ship bound to China, it has been planned between Elder Brother and my father Zendre Joshu to save me, to save the Brothers, and to save the Wisdom.

While I was asleep in a small free negotiated den, my locket's black crystal (a fragment of Philosopher's stone) inside started glowing brighter and brighter, which woke me up. Upon opening, visions filled my head, a lot of happenings...roaming black beasts, running in a pack with the speed unusual to men, black wolves resting under caves in a vast chamber, warmed by crystal fire. The scene draws farther away from the pack to the mouth of the cave, to the outside of the animal-shaped Howling Wolf Mountain. As it goes further away, I subconsciously visualized a vision of numerous humans mourning in unison honoring a major procession of a clan to the hill. The collective aura of the united clan cries for help, that's why the energy of the aura has found a fated god across the gateway. It exited through a transforming hovering solid rock structure gateway. It continued through the rock tunnel out to the crust upward to the ground surface, leading its way across the woods, to the village, and to the city, up to the seaport... and it reaches to connect to the Black Monolith inside my locket, beckoning!

The mourning tribe of the dying god predator, all perceived the vanishing glow of my aura.

I woke up from the vision; this time, I must slap my face to feel the real pain to justify I'm totally awake from my dream and not in my dream.

Zenie inside the ship has made clear the vision he saw needs his presence. It's telling him it's from someone that lived across the gateway, a hovering mysterious figurative solid rock structure. Abruptly, he remembered there was a light in his dream, the light that baffled him was coming from his locket, glowing like a pumping heart...drawing energy from somewhere. He opened the locket and there he saw a light manipulating his senses leading him outside the ship as he followed it through the hallway, up to the upper deck. He asked himself if people around could see the manifestation of light, a strand that continued to glow he clearly fathom he alone could see, off to the deck and along the dark surface of the sea.

He looked back around, and he heard something... there was this voice this time, a command, telling him a task to accomplish. But no one's behind him. A man is coming carrying a bucket with water, probably one crew, but he knew the distance wouldn't suggest the crew did it.

So, he thought of something clever, he asked the crew with the bucket to have a little water, to which he used to splash it on his face.

"Now I'm fully awake...but the whispering...authorizing me to do something!"

"I am the Fourth Realm...
The connection will do you no harm.
If the dead god's message is overlooked,
Don't deserve to plead upon… you coward spook!"

Despite feeling skeptical, I jumped over the ship, and swim a few meters, to where I followed the connection, it lets me reach a solid rock that only I could see in the very dark open water because of the help of the connection (the light). Followed the light and there I understood each step made, there were rock surfaces and shallow ground to reach the shoreline. Long story short, I arrived at the site of a wilderness and passed the city and the town.

"It's getting too dark in here," and I recalled when my father told me there's nothing to be afraid of in the dark, it's just the fear that spooks me out. And I whispered... "wait until your eyes could adapt to it and you can see."

The light I was following led me to a hole shaken by the quake due to the massive energy of aura from the crying clan of a god predator. I found out that without the guiding light, getting into the underground path would be inaccessible, dark as it goes down deeper into the ground that seems to open into a great ground tunnel. At the dead end, it's more like a chamber that could comprise an army of hundred. I noticed the dome-shaped chamber with a big block stone wall arranged neatly to be manmade like jigsaw, large bricks built out of quarried rocks from elsewhere. Although cracks were visible due to earth crust shifting and some root trees seeping through them, the only light that aids me is the thick strand connection and it continues to the opposite end of the dark chamber. I walked closer, following the countless strands of light, leading me to a focal structure that I had no idea what it was but only have seen hours ago in my vision. "It's a huge triangle structure but its base side has a gap in the center." By looking further and closer, its surface has minute inscriptions on them. "There must be something that I must figure out here...that seemly designed to give an intended purpose like going through..."

A few more seconds and it has caught my full attention, "the structure moves. Did I step onto something?" That scared me, that I might be buried down here alive! It detached itself away from the original wall. "... what the...hell, what did I just do!!" I flinched and moved backward with my awkward freaked-out face. It seems it is alive and followed me while I walked backward, and it suddenly stops at the center. It hovers in the middle of the chamber. "That was a relief."

The boundary between the human world to other worlds I seem to guess. I walk around to inspect it, but it followed my motion, it never stayed put in a position...I feel like it's reacting to my necklace...because it eventually defies the gravity my locket was drawn exactly pointing to the center of this giant whatever. I hear it hums like a machine, but it's no machine. The one thing in my vision...no one knows it had existed in the mainland, "I wonder why it opened with mystical divinity on me..."

In front of my marveling awakened senses, I can see through the gateway, and it isn't revealing the other side of the realm but the walls of the round chamber. When I am about to cross the realm gate with my locket, I could hear humming...getting stronger, slow and gentle, and pleasing. One thing drifted into my mind, the realm door that I went through when I was six reminds me that they are similar, only it is wider and this needs transformation until it stops to allow somebody to pass through, but only one thing in common with the two gates I just thought and theorized. They both need a philosopher stone to get through them, the Black monolith inside my locket.

Upon crossing, I encounter two colossal structures like obelisks with a height of almost four-story building standing side by side and on top of each sit giant sculptured Vampire wolves facing each other as if going on a fight.

I breathed in some air, "definitely I am in another world, complete with land terrain, giant trees, and starry purple sky."

The vast strip of land abounds with thick surmounting woods on the left, fruit trees on the right, and an infinite valley where more cultivated orchard trees are being grown. And it was so abrupt that I never paid attention to my time track, the sun started rising to where the Howling Wolf Mountain in the east is spotted!

I knew the feeling before, I'm worried not because of the pain experience, that I would bolt to anywhere in a strange land, but I don't have a log cabin to go to this time, "I'm a stranger here, don't even know their mores, their reaction to outlanders, their protocols and curfew of hours to be in and out of a shelter!" I was talking to myself. I'm going to be damned...only seconds away the sun is rising!

I'm about to protect myself with arms crossed over my face...

"Wait... I don't burn here...there's no pain at all!" I chuckled livelily and move on to where I wanted to go...I just recalled the strand of light is still connected to my necklace's locket.

I roam, but as I proceeded to more steps, I could perceive I'd been watched all around, but not realizing, the energy aura around me had transformed into a shape of a beast. And from it, the aura of my true form manifests around my young self...it's a tall giant wolf glowing in a golden flaming aura.

"I see strands of lights from every direction, but I don't see anybody!" I figured out, I tried to pick up some pace, my motion gets its speed, with that velocity, I started to see some predator creatures around me... they were human, the more I explore around, the gathering increased in volume.

Then I notice a huge gathering. And as I gets closer to the crowd, I realized it was a gathering of Vampire wolves in honor of a wolf god's funeral. I stopped advancing and had a frozen stare at the ceremony, and the whisper spoke to me. That's when I realized my purpose and the details about the people's cries in the form of aura light converged prevail. It continued to speak...

"Bring my body to the Fourth Realm and surrender it." Without assessing who just uttered the whisper, I leniently submit to it.

The procession advanced into the thick-walled fortress. From up view, the fort is in the form of two circular walls. No idea what the fortress hold, but the Vampire wolf clan calls it the Fourth realm, located uphill. Still frozen, I heard the same whisperer commanding...but in every line whispered, there is fulfilled reaction in my mind, perhaps the answer.

"He is the Fourth Realm!" My senses show a dark shadow of aura arising profusely from around the throne with blazing powerful darker eyes staring.

"Mourners need your bravery by all of 'em..." See myself carrying the dead body of their god, but another future vision shows the same crowd in support to lead a battle.

"Message of departed one was your vision," The scene brought me and the departed god predator into pure white dimension.

"Heed to their gathering to fulfill a critical point mission." The last line of the whisper depicted a huge gate with a bizarre inscription, "The Gate once open, has served its purpose...Accepting your risk!"

Zenie has conceptualized as he moves on to meet up with the family left by the apex predator god, the Vampire wolf god, despite he knew the cause of the Vampire wolf god's death...he risked himself to do the honor of handling their god's body inside the Fourth Realm.

Finally, I had thought it all, "the light...the strand of connection that leads me in this world is the converged *cries* of the people of the Vampire Wolf Chief god." I could see it clearly due to my hunting ground sight, the sensing bond other aurans call it. And the vision I had started in the ship...all those times it's the *message* of the Vampire wolf god, **it was him messaging me, even in his death...and now it's time to do my part for them.**

That experience has changed my concept regarding death as the end of existence, it's wrong, and I had proven it when I met face to face the one who calls himself the Fourth realm!

The widowed wife of the predator god, as I assumed, has prepared the dauntless hundred armies to go with the predator god. But as they march to carry the body, the son of the predator god, younger than me, calls her mother, and points at me. He has read my thoughts that I would do the handling over instead of sacrificing a hundred armies locked forever inside the Fourth realm.

I knelt before the god's wife, the deceased god's wife young and beautiful saw not a young brave, but an imprudent boy in front of her and among her people, but what all they flinched about is when my aura of flame was unconsciously revealed to all of them.

"I would take the predator god to walk the path into the Fourth realm in place of your hundred armies."

"Why do such a thing? Have you gone mad, stranger? You're not even one of his people, young foolish man!"

"Definitely not one of his people, but one god predator parallel to him!"

Instead of feeling bereaved, it turned her into raging at every uttered word I did. In sarcasm, the widow flaunted her majestic role as the god predator's wife. "If you cannot pass through me, you better decide to leave, for you have no idea what's on the other side of that Fourth Realm."

She mustered her assistants to suit her, bringing the armors, she emanated an aura to draw all the armors and completely dressed herself up clinging like a magnet armor on her arms, chest, shoulders, and waistline. Drawing her sword from an invisible sheath, it's the sword forged in that world. She charged so madly knowing the disrespecting behavior of the stranger.

From the ground, it seems Zenie wasn't moving but his dodges are remarkably fast enough to predict the exact hit of the widow.

"She's moving slow!" I moved around her, seeing her neck, her chest, the side of her waist, and her back. Her eyes perfected her beauty that I get distracted! And I was to cut in half her sword, she noticed, I realized her eyes reacted swiftly she doesn't want her sword scratch with my claws... why? And it turned out she'd laid cut on my deltoid, both arms.

The disputes of egos turned bland when Zenie god unnoticeably captured the sword of the widow but obtained cuts.

"Huh...where did my sword go; how did he seize it from me?" She halted, and from behind, god predator Zenie showed up from speeding.

"You are bleeding!" Impressed but ignoring to admit the boy has potential.

"You mean I'm healing! I have no intention of disrespecting god predator Goram's death and his people. I only come here to fulfill his wish, perhaps you can allow me now to take him to the Fourth Realm."

The widowed wife trembled but not in fear, she was just startled at the different level of aura I emanated. "My...god! With that aura of flame still soaring, he could turn an army of hundreds or thousands of my people in instant Vampire wolves, **his command of aura not even aware can persuade any predator to bow down."**

All the people of the Vampire wolf clan gave path to the brave young man Zenie as he carries the body of the Vampire wolf god. He recognized the right arm was decapitated. As he mourned too, his fiery aura grew stronger, wider in radius. He could hear a lot of mind whispers...

"Who is he...he's so powerful by the looks of the displayed aura...will he go alone inside...is he joking...maybe gone mad...he saves our people hundreds of them..."

Five feet away from the two heavy doors of the fourth realm, I saw an inscription not written by one of the people of the Vampire wolves. Querry in my head, another vision (the predator god's message) has ushered in while carrying the god's body. I saw how it was written, dark lightning from the dark sky in series, hitting the hard metal door. And the blazing scorch mark left the warning inscription, still smoking when a loud blaring trumpet was sounded and heard by the entire predator kingdom...not only the Vampire wolf clan but other predator clans as well. Then a god's voice, loud as the eruption of several volcanoes combined, gave a message to apprise them of the use of the built structure.

"Call it the Fourth realm, where only I could find sanctuary to meet up with your loved members. I will give them refuge, I am their god who will take in all their dark sides, even how heavily burden they are, their darkness will be mind. But I have a price to ask for everyone who enters, the deliverer and the body will be mine...to transcend them to my Twin brothers' sanctuary after I take out their darkness!"

Indeed, the first time I caught attention to the warning, I knew I would be locked in and never comes out, *"The gate, once open, has served one purpose...accepting your risk."*

The metal gate creaked...volatile air escaped from the opened gate. I walked in after several Vampire wolves pulled hard to open both heavy doors supported in long chains...and released to shut it behind me inside the dark fourth realm.

All that has happened to me, from the ship summoned by the vision of the late Predator god up to my dauntless encounter with the Dark god of the Fourth Ream transpired on the same day, but that day in the World of the Predator's kingdom, I, being inside the Fourth realm has taken me days to undergo, that's the power of the Fourth Realm culminated it to occur.

CHAPTER EIGHT

THE HUNTING SERPENT GOD

It started an overcast Friday morning, the boy Haniel arose from the dead using one soul and using the power of Creation, it's the same time when god predator Zenie entered the Fourth Realm and awaken Dark god Thaniel, wherein the time of days gets ahead, leaving Predators' Kingdom's time-period to move slowly, that Wednesday of twelve AM.

A couple of hours before Friday noon...

The departure was so utterly frustrating on the part of the Great Brothers of the Congregation, leaving the country empty-handed. The Brothers of Congregation never admit defeat; in the eyes of many in the court, they seemed to agree with the result, but the judgment never ends there...

Already far from the Wisdom domain of the Black Canis lupus, however, a few more kilometers before they reach the town proper, the four carriages halted by the side of the dirt road. The Chief Andra of the Congregation stepped out of his vehicle and gave an order to their realm god inside his own carriage, secretly disguised as one rich tourist venturing with his own vehicle with a hired coachman. The realm god has just arrived, the last resort to accomplish what isn't done by the Congregation.

"Bring home the evidence with all you might! I prefer dead...I will provide you the best serpent sorcerers to be your warriors...use them, control them to resume our plan." Commanding with exuberant rage, this is the order of the Chief Eldest of Congregation Andra, talking to a tall man cloaked in black red. His emblem on his cloak never appears unless a detected realm creature roams in a definite range near him. However, while still listening to the one ordering him, he slightly tilted his head, rolled his eyeballs, perceiving something familiar, the *scent* of a black gem or crystal of manipulation. He stepped out, nodded to the Congregation brothers, hats off slightly as the carriages left. From the back of his cloak, his infinity serpent symbol appears to respond in a glow apparently.

Three female sorcerers have also stepped out from their respective vehicles from his distance, walking towards him and gathering.

But in his critiquing mind, "yeah...your obsolete Congregation has never proven of anything, even blinded by these female serpent warriors on the fraudulence of your last witness. Now... you're putting the rest of your glorious plot in me, secretly and cowardly, without the knowledge of the Brotherhood, especially the Black Wolf region, so as not to start a war."

Despising the Congregation, "...you hypocrites...always want to be the first lead of the brotherhood...but you can't even handle your own war. What's so intriguing with Black Canis lupus Brotherhood anyway? It's nothing special. **They're just human who can be easily thoroughly trampled by god...whatever their source of strength is the same as their weaknesses, their love ones!!!**"

As they gathered all four, transposition has transpired in the process, comprising the dispersion of enormous black flaming aura from the god, which draws in the auras of the serpent warriors, making their heart, mind, and soul... as an empty slate.

"Oh, Dangerous Truth I come to Thee.
Clear the mind, heart, and soul of these three.
Engulf them with my aura,
And execute a will on behalf of me!"

"I baptized you with new names...from this day forth, use the power of that name bestowed on you, accordingly...Cecilia, my deceiver who can blind all senses, Lucy...the elucidator, keen observer, you will alarm me and report anything to me. And lastly, Jinx...you can cast a spell, curse, or deadly magic, but killing is under my permission."

Interrupted by his power of wide radius perception of the familiar scent of a manipulating crystal, he looked across the forest. "It's a boy," the god ordered at once the serpent warriors to pursue the perceived target. "He's carrying something's not from this world. Hurry...surround him, stop him...before he reaches home, and I'll catch up with you." And the three serpent warriors dashed towards the thick forest.

Back to Haniel's current situation, he walked straight home, but as the boy approaches the steps to the front porch, his senses came back. "Wicked," he said to himself, "did mom leave the house?"

Opening the door... wickedly, he felt something wasn't right, because the door opened by itself as somebody wants him in so quickly. Inside he walked with caution, and he even takes hold of a hard wooden rod to defend himself. He found his mom tied to a dining chair in the kitchen, he rushed with a racing heartbeat to untie her poor mom. "Who did this to you, mom?"

He felt someone walking behind him nearing, the sound on the floor squeaking. When the boy turned to vigorously hit whoever was behind him, the rod was blocked by a strong handgrip unsuitably belonging to a beautiful young woman who afterward unveiled her dark red cloak to introduce herself.

"Is that how your mother taught you how to treat a young woman like me, or perhaps you're just nervous it's your first time seeing a pretty girl in front of your mom?" She playfully turned the rod into a snake which jumpscares the boy.

"Jinx!" Yelled Cecilia. "That's my name! I bring spell and misfortune magic." Answered Jinx in a flaunting voice to the boy as she offered back his wooden rod.

Cecilia interrupted; she appears through the breeze and manifested into her flesh, "will you be nice to him? I'm Cecilia, blame me for misleading your senses...just doing what I was ordered to...to deceive and blind my victim."

Lucy and Jinx fuse magic and illumination, the old country house by their farm turned into an abandoned ruin brick and with partial falling roof in front of the boy's wondering blown mind.

"Where's the house? Where's my mom?" Astonished as the boy reacted.

"Sorry dear, there never was a house nor your mom... you've never actually reached your home and your mom. We're in the middle of the forest...here in this abandoned, filthy abode. We have hypnotized you and led you here. That's why you probably wondered you felt weird when you get to the familiar place, and they seemed to appear different." Explained Lucy as she introduced herself, "I'm Lucy, gifted with illumination and clarification to those who are misled by wrong sensing.

Cecilia smiling, did a little blinding illusion to renovate the ruin and the dilapidated roof into better descent English shelter...and she patted her hands together as if she meant a piece of cake magic! And she answered the boy, we are miles away from your house, and your mom is safe...now show us the locket you found in the woods!"

The boy looks at them one by one, "I don't know what you are talking about, miss..."

"Oh yes, you do; once I will put a curse on your mom," as she started to turn from them to exit and to disappear.

"Please...don't, please don't!!! Begged the boy. Jinx reappears.

Then Serpent god gets into the house. He walks as he is looking straight at his victim...and as he gets closer to the boy, his victim's eyes reflect what the realm god looks like while emanating his black aura surrounding the god. As he came nearer, the boy really got frightened as he fainted while seated on the chair.

"I don't want to hurt you, boy, we are no match "...and in a blink of an eye, Serpent god gazed in his hand at the pendant necklace of the black locket and had it closer to the boy's face. He snapped his finger to awaken the boy's mind, although weird as it looks because the reason is responding, but his senses are totally unconscious.

"Where have you gotten this, boy?" He draws back the spiritual soul of the boy back to his physical body by a wave. The boy awakens.

The boy hesitated to answer because he believes it was precious and from where he found it, there might be more...that's what the boy wants them to read in his mind.

The Serpent god has read his mind and sought what causes the stalling, but the god just knows exactly how to persuade him. He walks around him, toying him like his prey, as he resembles the slithering snake keeping his face close to the boy's, looking him in the eyes. The boy saw auran images that came out from the Serpent god, three humongous snakes but pretended he can't see them.

"You know what...there's more of those where you have found it. We won't get this locket from you; there's more of the gem buried close by. Bring us there, and you will have tons of gems to bring home to your mom. This day forth...your life's been changed to forever greatness."

"Just say yes...I will cooperate." The god whispered that to the boy. He walked three steps away from him, tilted his head like a snake, stretching. "Even if you don't cooperate, I have the power to reverse that phenomenon." He stretches his arms next as if he's going to do a fervent transposition.

The auran snakes coiled around the sitting boy acting that he has no idea how he's levitated, even though he could obviously witness the manipulated aura in the form of snakes lifting him up. "I can control life...I can control minds...I can alter your temperament, your rage...your discomfort, but when I do that, you will regret it, I would ask for a bigger price, perhaps the dearest to you as of now...so think it over."

"But if I can persuade you easily without needing all the things I've said, then would simply say... bring us to where we are supposed to be, as in now!" Yelling the boy while again emanating his enormous black waving upward auras.

Few more minutes, and they're brought to the site where the boy found the black locket.

The expression on the face of the god was astounding, believing and feeling the site has the energy that induces and augments his strength. "We are truly here," he faces the three serpent warriors with evil contentment and ordered them urgently, "spread out, and if you've sought it, call without speaking!"

By that order, the boy rest assured that he can get a better deal with the help of the god and his apprentices.

Further later, the Serpent god found the opening and descends to the ground opening. He raised both his hands slowly and calmly right in front of his chest and stared at them until both hands ignited to flame. Then, he walks inside the underground dirt tunnel bored by the projectile energy, until he reaches the vast dome chamber.

Calling without speaking, the Serpent god was standing before the Gateway, no idea it's an Ancient Gadi Trinity symbol in a dome huge chamber occupied by hanging tree roots but previously burnt. But the triangular gate (Ancient Gadi Trinity) has been moved to the center, already levitating, which means that a black gem, the only key held in a locket is close nearby.

Astonished and wondering, despite the different shape and form of the Realm gate, he entered through, and the familiar Predator's kingdom was made known to his sight and memory. He pondered, "I knew this place, but I have entered a very different Realm gate."

When the three serpent warriors heard of their god's calling without speaking, they walked through the dirt tunnel. Behind them was the boy following all in his trembling and fearing consciousness. They all saw the Serpent god's left hand in a flame while, on the other hand, holding the black locket by the chain upon reaching the dead end and witnessing the phenomenon of the locket being drawn forward. His back cloak symbol is more striking. He walked slowly towards it, and the black locket being pulled forward phased through the other side. He has concluded that whatever the locket's components he's holding must be the key to allow anybody to get through it.

He looked closer, as his eyes followed the feel of its touch. However, upon touching the structure, a vision responded to his consciousness. The staggering visions that came into his mind were the black wolf riders, three of them going in and out... a hooded young man shrouded with dark shadows walking along with him with a flaming fiery aura. But there's more to the vision feeding his mind, it's scheming persons who are related to the three wolf riders. And the weakest has been selected amongst his targets... not Alexis, the loser old friend of Brother Narija, stalking someone in the dark alley, not the twelve warriors of the realm door, including Elder Brother, but the wife of Brother Zendre. She's all alone in the house during the night, unprotected.

"So that's how Black Wolf brotherhood is exceptional..." And he goes through the gateway. The hovering gate move to the wall and embedded itself and solidified with the wall as part of it.

The three serpent warriors waited with the young boy behind them, smiling as he curved his lips slightly. A few more seconds and the Ancient Gadi Trinity symbol (the gate) by the wall detached itself and hovered again in the middle, their Serpent god stepped through the gate, and uttered greedily, "I have found the evidence, Black Canis lupus Brotherhood will be mine! Get rid of the boy, divide his soul among you three, and leave his body to rot." The Serpent god commanded, and the boy started screaming as the three serpent warriors tear his soul to be divided among them.

That evening in town, a stalking man in pursuit of another man whom he had witnessed had barged into the house of Dr. and Mrs. Zendre Joshu. While the stalker is waiting for the intruder to come out in the dark alley, the time has lapsed that he never saw him exit to the same door. He insistently waited for more time until the man he was waiting for came down unnoticed while descending creepily from the midair behind the stalker, with his black aura outpouring profusely like it's propelling the man to defy gravity.

He walked unnoticeably from behind the stalker in the dark alley, and startle the man, "are you waiting for someone?"

The god simply reads mind... ready to control, use, or even kill the man after what may come out of his assessment of his stalker. Besides reading, the god has obtained all the connections, the stalker's past with an old childhood friend, the orphanage where their friendship originated, and how those friendships crumbled because of insecurities, jealousy, and greed or ambition.

"Alexis Fortuni... 'been brewing very harmful revenge on one member of the three wolf riders...Brother Narija Martin!"

"I am thinking of feeding your soul to my three warriors, but I've changed my plan...because you meant to kill and not meant to be killed." The stalker has no idea of what had awfully committed in the house of Dr. Zendre.

He didn't kill anyone yet, but the woman inside Dr. Zendre's house is connected to the Serpent god's soul... "that whenever I die in the fight with anyone supporting the Black Wolf brotherhood, there's collateral!"

CHAPTER NINE

A STREET FIGHT

Around nine pm, Friday...

Zenie always checks up on her mom, knowing she's all alone. But like a thief in the night, he has never noticed anyone break into their house. As he double-checks every window and door, all is usual, with no signs of force. But he still can feel someone with power, despite, what he described there's blurriness, like messing up with his mind and senses, doubting that something's roaming and lurking around.

That's because it was specified by the encountered dark god Thaniel and the calm god Haniel back in the Fourth Realm, that I have transcended, but not knowing I couldn't apply any more of any senses to perceive dangers. It now became the Twin gods in the Fourth Realm merged within me are the judges of any impending dangers.

Haniel spoke in my head, "I want to go hunt that kid who stole my key necklace!"

Thaniel keeps interrupting his twin brother, "I prefer to pick a fight with someone corrupt and wicked, the worst, the better."

Then Haniel directly cleared my doubts speaking inside my head, "Zenie, chosen god by the Predator's kingdom, it would be hard for you to be identified by any lower god below the Fourth Realm!"

"Why?" I asked even though a relevant notion formulates in my mind.

"Your auras even when you get emotionally overwhelmed...won't emanate but you can still manipulate them. We are now that aura that you have, the *darkest* and most *tranquil* and very uncanny to humanity.

No lower than me can see it coming...unless I am not within you!" The Fourth Realm gods themselves explained.

I observed how mother feels at home and cozy, and before I have to leave her, gave her a hug and kiss, and concerned, "do you feel anything unusual around you, mom?"

"You are...with extreme wit, as we both can tell, but too nervous as you may appear. What's bothering you, my boy?"

"I can sniff something isn't right, but nothing I can see and know to prove it."

After all, Zenie's inference is right, there's something that he could sense but cannot pinpoint.

After he's gone, Lucy appears first, dispersing all the concealment of deceptions (done by Cecilia) as the other two serpent warriors reappear in their usual images, and including the real mother of Zenie, as controlled in every way with her shut mind and senses. Still moving and walking around the house with the three servants of the realm god, the mother has no reaction to everything, not even complaining. But the one thing they can't do to her is by putting a Deadly curse to kill her.

The very young and pretty serpent warrior, Jinx chortled with joy and with a killer smile, kept teasing the two.

"That's relieving that he's gone, but ironically, I still want his warm hug, so strong and robust muscles I still could feel it...it has tickled me up to my bones!"

"Enough of your fantasy, already, Jinx...but well done, you did there... acting like his mother. But we're not done yet!" Cecilia is imposing everyone to get back to work.

Lucy intervenes... "are you still fantasizing about Zenie? You're not his type?"

"I'm going to curse you the most humiliating and the slowest painful death never occurred to human nerves and senses...retract what you have said, at once, Lucy!" Reacted quickly with agitation.

"Okay...okay, I'm just telling the truth to you. It's not my call to bring lies and deceit...my god me!" She rolled her eyeballs.

For the time being, the Serpent god and Alexis had their stroll in town, heading to a bar. The night's still young, perfect to complete their night's agenda against the three black wolf riders, knowing that they must be crippled, which has been the god's plan to renew and control the black wolf brotherhood.

At 10 PM, I accidentally run into the Serpent god and Alexis. But with Haniel and Thaniel, Haniel has certainly recognized the face and voice of the taller man that belittled him and immediately ordered with vengeful connotations me to follow them. "Zenie, put on your hoody."

"That's the guy I've been telling you earlier, it disgusts me when I recall what that Serpent god, together with the three female supporters, did to me!"

They walked by each other side by side, and Zenie rolled his eyes, the peripheral vision looks as he walked past his target. He never loses sight of the Serpent god, and the Fourth Realm gods surprise Zenie with their next move. They call out designedly the Aura of Flesh to turn Zenie into someone else... become Haniel in identity. A sudden transfiguration of Zenie's face with a bright aura dispersal had occurred.

Nervous but ready, I knew I am protected by the twin brothers, tagging along within my body and mind, I got the feeling that human gods are below us, I am a human god, but now I could experience how to react and counteract by not being identified as me. And we confronted the Serpent god.

"Hey, I know you. You're the man who has my necklace...you've forgotten to return it after we've found that mysterious ancient gateway."

"Sorry, kid...you've mistaken me for someone else." That bastard spoke at me with confidence, just like that, no way he could just proceed with what he wished tonight!

I insisted, even disrespectfully pulling his coat by the arm. "No, I thought your Congregation brothers have left this morning. Are you intending to stay in town just because you've found a mystical gateway that goes to the supernatural world? Give me back my locket, mister!"

He glared at me after stretching neatly and shrugged his shoulder. Yelling. "Get lost, kid! I don't know what you're babbling about." His mind played along how on that moment at the chamber when he ordered the three Serpent warriors to tear down the boy's soul...could someone be back to life? "Did the three disobey my order?" He reflected on what transpired in the chamber.

I was just observing, understanding Haniel...when he decided to resurrect his decayed body that rested for centuries, his necklace that kept the Black Fragment of the Monolith also resurfaced from underneath the ground. Waiting for Haniel's further action, I really think that Haniel is pissed.

"Now I will give that Serpent man-made god a lesson!" His rage escalated.

Concerned for his younger twin brother, Thaniel asks, "Haniel if there's something you want, there's no need to hesitate. I have many allies of darkness that I can resurrect since the early civilizations started."

"Just stay put brother Thaniel, this is my fight tonight. If I need you, you can rumble accordingly and freely!"

I stayed quiet while listening to the great words of the great gods, not even reacting nor interrupting...moreover, I'm learning what powers are about to be disclosed by the twin gods. "This is going to be fun and dangerous!"

The power of transformation created by the twin gods within him summons the power of Creation, meaning the Aura of flesh. Power of Creation uses the Aura of Flesh (anything organic dead or alive), mimicking what's on the ground and every living creature. Power of Devastation uses the Aura of Temper, the fire, or water. And the Power of Possession uses the Aura of Psyche, the air, possessing any creature in mind and body.

Alexis and the god went inside the bar, ordered a drink, and began to exchange talks. Alexis remains quiet but keenly deductively observing and pondering about the god's power in front of him. Thinking about how he might use a god's power to do him a favor for his personal problem.

"Are you the realm god from the Congregation? It seems that boy knew something about you and what you did to him." Alexis holding a glass of whiskey on the rock.

"Yes...I am what you think I am. Disguised in your world to say... explore my great power of potential, although as of now, I might probably double that chance... since the boy you heard of what he was claiming from me is all true. I have discovered a source of power hiding underground in the forest, deep underground...and I want you to explore it with me."

He sighed with relief for he didn't expect the god's response would be like that. "That's why I came to see you!" Alexis was more to expect him to be bossy and impatient and could anytime choke him to death.

"Or should you say...you've been stalking or sneaking on my back! Well, with your extra help, my plan to lock them up, the Elder brother and his two friends on the other side of the realm gate would take shape, and the Brotherhood's domain will be renewed and be mine." He opened his fist as he savors the moment of enjoying how great to have a key in his hand (the black locket), holding a greater future.

After taking another gulp from his glass, Alexis gave his intoxicating idea of revenge. "As your servant, my men and I will join your group of mercenaries, in exchange for one thing, to put down Brother Narija.

Reading the mind of the pathetic stalker, the Serpent god has driven to impart what he plotted to do during the infiltration of the Predators' kingdom. For he not only wins to see the three black wolf riders in their failure, but he could also transcend to a more Omni god greater than any endowed human as realm gods.

"Watch and digest what you're going to behold...I, too, do not know this plan I'm about to take if not with the three Realm knowledge that circulates my brain as a living three souls."

"If you wish to partake with my generosity, take the opportunity to embrace my invitation and you will not only avenge for your lowly defeated esteem against your childhood rival. You will go far looking down at him with his underlying disappointment."

Haniel speaking in a godly voice. "My twin brother Thaniel bestowed me beforehand a heads up that the first group of guys that I would be encountering are from the Congregation with powers of the Deadly. With darkest intentions, darker than the order of the Eldest Chief Andra, I know my brother knew me for being obstinate because I have my own decision, when I don't listen, I put my head into 'sleep' mode, the Deep slumber...I become more aware, though."

"I don't want to apply the word 'dead' because Thaniel**, my twin brother, and I don't rest in peace forever...we watch in peace, and if it's a must we get a war to deliver peace!** We linger in our limitless immeasurable abode, the Fourth Realm, wider and better than humans' surface world. But because one incredibly brave young man name Zenie has opened his surface world with us, and because Thaniel longed to see the surface world again, I committed to tag along with them, so both Thaniel and I share with Zenie's physical body and mind, not the soul. In return and in power, either one of us can conceal the enormous god predator aura of Zenie whenever his emotion goes into raging, so no Deadly user can identify him...because 'We' promise to keep him safe in return for my brother Thaniel's wishes.

I've been 'asleep' in my sanctuary for centuries, still fresh in my memory about my past knowing that humans in this surface world would have changed but not to my meticulous observation, and I have to require a taste of my gift right now in the middle of the humans...in one city of England."

"I am going to pick a street fight tonight and see how it will go." And so, in front of the bar across the street where the two (Alexis and the Serpent god) are plotting their converging tactics against conquering Predators' kingdom and overtaking the Brotherhood of the Black Wolf, I told my non-reluctant twin brother, ready in hot to gear up his lending hand.

The eerie tone in my senses played, and slightly looked down glaring upon the unaware Serpent god, with closed fists and closed eyes...my clenched fists opened, but both eyes turned bright white almost like the eyes of a blind man...the glowing aura of senses started from my eyes crawling... igniting every cell to fiery white flame...and reaches my open hands, and when the power of the Calming aura reaches the ground, it fanned out a wave around me viewed from up above.

All who have been reached by the wave of my Deep slumber would go unconscious. I was aware of my intention, that I don't want them to see, and experience how terrifying it would be. The power of the deep slumber is for the people around (and not for me) to steer clear of panic!

And so it began, including Alexis losing the grip of his whiskey, the bartender serving in front, all dropped to unconsciousness.

"What the hell happened to him?" Serpent god gave thought to what happened to Alexis. Then sounds of clashes outside the street greatly alarmed him to walk out that door.

"I've been to several sites of war, where I blend within the vicinity, and no one could see me come up, but this time, I can tell clearly that I stood out from the rest of what's happening."

His notion was true. There's one young man with an unknown identity standing facing him, He lighted up a cigarette to build a time to get to know the young man, "I can now recall, he's the persistent boy who attempted to ruin my night an hour ago."

The heaven that turned into dark clouds brought forth lightning not the average ones seen during a storm. Standing in the middle of the street Haniel's both arms were struck by the summoned lightning, equipped his arms with gauntlets, and then the following lightning hits the ground, impaled by his Reaping sword. Glass windows shattered, flipping in mid-air even shattered the second time into smaller pieces.

Zenie has acknowledged the unbelievable, as Haniel said, "ignore my friend, more of these will happen in the future." Zenie replied with a simple but shivering yes, he knew Haniel's more than capable to teach what he is about to witness.

From place to place in my five-mile radius, all infrastructures from power plant generators, telecommunication, and all kinds of transportation, were wrecked into chaos. Train speeding derailed, gas stations exploded, all because everyone around the range distance of Haniel went to a very deep slumber. Power outage came along next....and from a wider perspective from above, water from rivers and seas began draining.

Serpent god didn't look around but took a pause to assess his enemy. He yelled from across the street. "I got the message, already whoever you are! But I would be fair to you...**it's not a shame to back off...more when you can't handle what you've started!** Did you get my message, young man?"

I squinted my eyes, I want to teach this kid, thinking straight that I won't let this slip away. **"In every fight...ego, arrogance, and ascertaining collide, which one are you, Sira alias Wedj?"** His eyes grew spooky after hearing his name. "You still don't get it, do you?" Those are the final judging words that came out from Haniel before he signed Thaniel to get ready. And from behind Sira, three alchemy circle doors appear, he had summoned his three serpent warriors.

After all the ruins have been flattened into rubbles, "There's no point of telling you this Sira, you did fight well, fighting me as your enemy, but I fought you not Haniel summons more of the flashes of lightning to pour down the city, one by one the building started collapsing, but nobody noticed even Zenie that all the unconscious and the three Serpent warriors had vanished, it's when Haniel let go of Twin Thaniel to stay in the reality with the three Serpent warriors, while He and Serpent god stayed put in a world called Construct, a replica of the city but not real.

Haniel has the power of not only manipulating the aura, but can replicate a venue, manipulate the time, the people's death and resurrection, the atmospheric pressure, and underneath the ground.

At the sudden disappearance of both Haniel and the Serpent god,

"Where are we? Jinx asked Lucy?" Where did the outraging young man and the boss go?"

Lucy responded confidently. "Just an ambiance manipulation."

"Get ready girls, this is not a time to discuss," Cecilia and her team have witnessed with caution one teenage girl resurrecting from unconsciousness, though unaware it's Thaniel, using Auran of Psyche, his soul has possessed teenage girl.

"Good I have left boss Sira, one Deadly mimicked auran image of me, just in case."

With Haniel's furious thought, "you think I died when you left my body at the chamber to rot..." He advances and vanished, and emerged again but has already leaped up high, released his Reaping sword straight toward his enemy's chest...but all of a sudden, Haniel couldn't believe, the swords stopped in the middle like something invisible has been hit, until he realized that Sira has armed himself with his three big auran images of serpents despite invisible to them because Haniel is merged to Zenie's...and the fact that Haniel isn't in a deep slumber. Same with Zenie he couldn't see the auran images being cast by the enemy.

"I have an idea Zenie, just follow my lead..." Both Haniel and Zenie saw the *Reaping sword* being pulled out by an unseen auran and was plunged to pierce a farther ground. They pretended to get to the sword but luring Sira's serpent to move away from its master, the serpents coiled Haniel's limbs closely tight to his body, which nearly choke him to death, his eyes shutting to pass out...but despite all that, deep in his thought, "just the way I planned it, Zenie."

Sira, smirking while pulling out the reaping sword, read an inscribed line on the sword. "...so, you're a reaper, but sadly I'm going to use your sword to reap your soul."

Now Zenie, suffering the same agony of being crushed to death, must follow his instinct to save themselves both. Shaking off the possessing soul of Haniel from his mind and body, the aura of the image of the Vampire wolf burst into flame! Zenie's agility was regained..making the serpent's squeezing grip loosen while Zenie took pleasure in running away, seeing the auran image of two serpents squirmed.

Sira is deemed confused. "What!? An auran manipulator like me?" As perceived by Sira the boy's nowhere to be found, while still holding the reaping sword, Sira panicked of Zenie's intermittent vanishing motion (the way of the vampire). That has sustained him too many injuries...surprised grabbed from the back, lift and slam, punched and jabbed, and clawed everywhere until Zenie took the opportunity to steal the sword from him.

Outsmarted, Sira reacted angrily. "I lost sight of the sword! Where did it go?!" It's the cue when Haniel took back to possess Zenie with the reaping sword. Back together again, Haniel flaunted a sword stance... open his silvery blind white eyes and yelled "Deep slumber!!!" More thunderbolts poured down wherever Haniel go this time, and his zigzag in slow-motion has driven Zenie to enjoy viewing synchronized downward strikes of the bolts of lightning. "Zenie, focus on me...we're on to eliminate the last auran serpent!"

Sira spoke to Haniel, "I don't care if you can hear me, but I'm sure you do, you're a god and yet you have no second thought of eliminating my auran images..."

"Don't you know who I am? I reap souls...remember when you left me in the chamber of the gate, ordered your warriors to tear down my soul among them? That was me!!" With that claim, the more Sira got pissed. He turned his remaining aura into a weapon, it physically manifested in his grip, an ax made from his symbol, the rod with intertwined serpents where the wings transfigured into blades (the Caduceus).

The battle between them never involved Zenie, because before they could have their duel, Zenie knew by the amount of aura emanating from Sira, that his aura won't last, eventually be devoured by the energy it uses, and would give in even before the duel ends.

After all the ruins have been flattened into rubbles, "There's no point of telling you this Sira, you did fight well, fighting me as your enemy, but I fought you not as my enemy but for me to take your soul out of miseries you have garnered along your ways, to prepare a pure consciousness for the next."

Haniel walked closer to Sira gesturing his one hand he won't fight no more and his other hand on his chest coughing off blood, he's down on his knees grunting almost to asphyxia, Haniel came to stop to heal him, and when it was over Haniel expected for the necklace, he turned and run, but the swift Vampire wolf Zenie anticipated, and shove his clawed hands before Sira realized, snatched the heart... "I've seen some flaws during our fight, like planets that orbit in a circle, we will repeat this over and over... till we meet again..." And Sira vanished as ashes blown, it was the mimic auran prepared by Cecilia.

On the other hand, Thaniel lets his action do the talking, he attacked the first warrior whom he knew is their leader, for the two younger warriors listen to what she said. He ran with the speed they haven't seen before, and surprisingly emerge from nowhere but above Cecilia, and stretch out his right hand from under where the alchemy circle seems to comply with his command, procuring Thaniel with a weapon, his favorite double-blade ax.

And before Jinx and Lucy could ever blink to realize, Thaniel's double ax has already been hooked to Cecilia's head...Thaniel as a little teenage girl watches the two very carefully, although Thaniel's reflexes move a thousand times faster than the two deadly.

The very slight movement has been detected, the hold of breath, the blink of the eyelid, the sudden change of their heartbeat. Without remorse, the teenage girl (Thaniel) swings to decapitate Cecilia's head.

"What shall we do, Lucy? This girl is a monster...what just happened to Cecilia?"

Lucy was enraged and her eyes are on the girl ten meters from them. And she's coming again. Abruptly, explosives were detonated as Thaniel comes in hot and with intent, dodging all the mine bombs planted by Lucy earlier, the one big explosive was directly below them.

"We all die in here together!" Lucy clenched her teeth. She yells. "Jinx suit yourself with armor now!!!"

Jinx looked at Lucy in fluctuating manner. "What the hell is she talking about?" Lucy repeated in mind whisper.

By the time Thaniel stepped into their ground, an uproar of big explosions blasted. They both had evaded the burning explosion planted by Lucy. That's because she armed herself with her gauntlet designed by their Congregation's military school. She formed her fist into rock and aimed at Jinx, an aura of a cannonball of rock pushed Jinx farther to safety. Upon landing, the two serpent warriors regroup, and out of their awareness, a wreck of a London downtown bus was thrown at them, Jinx did a hand gesture of spreading a wider door in the mid-air to catch the incoming falling big object coming through them. "Hurry up you tenacious bitch, did you run out already?!"

They saw the teenage girl crawling half bodied, and only did she stop when a black aura burst from the body...the ax dissipated.

Lucy can feel Jinx's infuriation, she's more on to violence. And she created more alchemy circles ready to shoot directly positioned at the darkened spectral.

They watch the giant black spectral shrink into a shadow of the human form. The two warriors were multiplied into several Jinx and Lucy clones, just in case.

"That's my final show ladies. Even if I accidentally kill you, I can resurrect you, the messing up with your time is done, because I am waiting for my twin brother's mind whisper, and it so happened his fight with your boss is over."

"Don't feel you're defeated, your other comrade is alive, had escaped before I beheaded her." The two were left muttering together glaring at their unknown opponent who just vanished.

CHAPTER TEN

VISIONS, CONNECTIONS, AND COMMAND

The previous battle between Haniel and Sira has gained benefits on the part of the god predator Zenie. If only fighting to the end is what matters, the soul-reaper gods would triumph in any kind of fight, but it's not what Haniel is after...besides retreating is still considered a tactic in every fight.

However, comes midnight...

And the last three riders of the twelve Black Wolf warriors proceeded as they plan to rendezvous at the open hollow ground aka the Ground portal that leads to the ancient tunnel. Out of the enemies' awareness... the three riders weren't the three wolf riders they were expecting. Those were the last three black wolf warriors on their horses: namely Hans, the Ax thrower, Pike, the Quick Archer that never aims, and Zohr, the Spear fighter sneaking into the darkness of the woods against the enemies. This was the plan instructed by their leader, Elder Brother at the Realm table, Friday afternoon.

And a flashback scene was conceptualized by Elder Brother while conducting a meeting assembly at the Realm table:

It was when those resentful (Wisdom trial) nights when the three brothers of the Brotherhood had found mitigating solutions- the summoning by the mysterious hooded man (god predator Zenie) to come over to the Predators' kingdom.

Synchronized queries were asked by Elder Brother, and Brother Narija, including Brother Zendre.

"Are you telling us god predator that your visions are the cry messages sent by the deceased god predator? Are these prophesied visions need our necessary action? For what reason do they need crucial attention, and intended solution?"

Elder Brother imparted and has explained everything from the summoning of the god predator (unidentified in the Realm table assembly) to the Congregation leaving their hunting Realm god, the prophesied visions of god predator, and up to the mission of the ten Black wolves during the meeting at the Realm table.

"We began to discern that the Brotherhood of Alchemy and Wisdom is at stake, meaning we can either lose or win in this war."

Hans, the Ax thrower... wanted to clarify, "but we already have won the Wisdom trial, even the son of Dr. Zendre Joshu had partaken their stupid Wisdom trial and proved nothing...resulting that the kid is wiser than them." The majority laughed at the imaginable insult made by the kid.

"What else do the Congregation want from us?" Asks Pike, the Archer that never aims.

Elder Brother started with a metaphor, "**The snakes have slithered away leaving its victim with a sting and venom.** By that I'm referring exactly to the Serpent congregation leaving us with a bigger problem, their Realm god, he is a hunter and a Deadly user."

Brother Narija was called by Elder Brother to stand and elaborated on what they have learned from their source, the mysterious hooded man who once came one night to share his plan to defeat their Serpent enemies.

Brother Narija stood...

"It's the prophesied visions that scare us, it doesn't matter how and who send to us, what we need is how to stop it. One of the three visions has already transpired.

Everyone seriously reacted upon hearing, "...that the Serpent god has managed to acquire a philosopher's stone, a key to the gateway.

"What are the two remainings?"

"He's going to find out if we are appealing aid illegally from any realms' kingdom...and lastly to prove a bloodline unofficially gifted with realms' ability."

"You might want to ask if we have somebody in the Brotherhood who might have broken such rules?" Elder Brother quickly answered his question. "Theoretically we don't."

"And how can the Serpent god accomplish those?"

"By entrapment, making her spy warriors blend in with you guys.

That's why be very perceptive on your way tomorrow night into the gateway...the Deadly users can copy each of you and blend so easily."

Brother Narija's next account overwhelmed everyone, "**I don't know if the following would strengthen or weaken you, but we are in this situation as a pack of wolves.** Elder Brother confirmed that no one in this room and in this Brotherhood has ever broken the rules assumed by their god, but if we can't prevent their god to manipulate Deadly, their god's immense power of entrapment can turn the table!"

"Elder Brother, what does the god predator have exactly in mind that he wanted us to do?" Suzu, the Quick sword, the in-charge, chosen by Elder Brother, inquires.

"Tomorrow...Friday midnight, ten of you will assemble at the Ground portal. You will march and head to the Howling wolf mountain, it is your duty to be inside the vast hollow mountain and search for the Transcending altar."

"Do we have any sketch of what it looks like, how big or small is this structure? Or any landmarks to identify?" Willy the Big sword requested.

"There is something," Elder Brother glanced at everyone waiting for his answer, "it is in the form of a triangle! A structure of an ancient."

"Triangle?" And someone elaborated further, "yeah like the shape of the roof of the house." Shun the Sword and dagger, replied.

The triangle. The first question that came up to my attention and to my insight is the Triangle structure, on how it does work to help in the transmutation process, called the Transcendence of the god. Elder Brother recalled while conveying in the Realm table gathering.

"Gentlemen, the Transcendence of the god, when that happens, the Predators' kingdom and our Brotherhood of Alchemy and Wisdom will be saved."

One from the Realm table exactly asked the same question I asked the god predator, the summoner of the Three Brothers that took place the night before Brother Narija is called for cross-examination in the trial.

"What if we find the Triangle structure? Can the god do the transcendence right away?"

"The answer to that question falls when a young lad had visualized a vision lively in his dream. He was leaving his country, his beautiful city, and his town, as a sacrifice in exchange to steer clear of subjugation. No choice but to leave his agonizing family from separation."

"While asleep, the vision that he knew was a dream, wasn't anymore. It's the cry of the future people that he would become, sent as luminescence in strand form collectively arranged by the deceased god to the next chosen god."

"Where are we?" The young boy who would become the next god predator looked around the pure white ambiance asks the only creature who was ahead of him in the vicinity. *"This is your dream,"* the retiring old god and dying turned to face the young lad, answered. He flinched at the fierce look of the god predator, *"Sorry to startle you, but I must transform into a human."*

"I am Goram, the god predator of the kingdom you had entered, when I had sniffed you, I knew you were young and vicious and tenacious, that's how I was taught in my world. So, I have to stop you, do a pinching bite on your neck and shoulder to get you unconscious. I'm sorry and when the door opened up again, I had to drag you hastily using my claws on your chest."

"I've learned how to transcend myself to a god that will save both my people in the kingdom and on the surface world."

-Zenie, The Young God Predator

Goram continued to talk to me in my vision. *"It's not in my position to ask, but upon meddling with the voices of the Twin of the Fourth Realm, I may need your help to save my Kingdom and my people."*

"And to fulfill the first request, you must attain to have transcendence, a transmutation by the help of the luminescence of the triangle."

"Fulfilling the first request by attaining transcendence granted by the judging gods of the Three Realms, you must get the knowledge of the light of the triangle by dealing with the most sinister attitude of the Twin of the Fourth Realm by surrendering my body. Saying, only in the presence of the Fourth Realm gods who would possess can procure the lights of the triangle."

"I call upon you through the cries of my people to relieve the position, and it so happened that my transmutation process wasn't responded by the three realm kingdoms when I attempted a calling at the Transcending altar. But the three realm doors to form the luminescence of triangle (triangle of light) didn't open up for me. Don't know why but that made me upset until my underlying conditions devoured my Omni power, my speed had weakened, and I slowed down to my very last breath."

Young god predator Zenie speaking of the plan... (This has never been imparted in the meeting at the Realm table).

The secrets in between the mission...the entrapment. In the continued planning of strategy with the Brothers, "three days from now, at midnight Elder Brother, you and your warriors will help me execute the whole process. The majority of your ten Wolf warriors' tasks is to lure our enemies and their god."

"But god predator, is that risky for my men if they intend to search something, and without their knowing an ambush comes attacking from elsewhere?"

"Entrapment is at its best objective when the hunters of the prey didn't know they're part of the game, that makes the luring very realistic. But I will merge my unanticipated plan to hold everything in place."

"You mean to use these men as bait, they have families too, for brother's sake!!!" The father reacted as his heightened temper couldn't swallow that notion his son has planned. And walk a distance away.

Brother Narija instilled a scene that might happen to the entrapment, "what if (inhale) the Deadly users succeed to blend with our ten Black wolves...and what if a majority of our warriors spotted them?"

"I saw that coming, brother Narija. Even I already have glimpsed how it would end, you are not god to know the truth in advance, the human mind can easily be distracted, but when it comes to focusing, it is infinite soaring."

They walked outside the mountain, the sun shines that afternoon breeze, and under the orchard trees, they walk through them with underlying branches full of slumbering buds that begin to bloom waiting for the right time of the season.

"Elder Brother, I want you to create a massive exact replica of the Howling wolf mountain, inside and outside." Elder Brother took a beautiful sight of the Howling wolf mountain, as Zenie pointed at it, "and that original beauty will be concealed in your ambiance manipulation, where you three would be watching every move of our warriors. Can you, do it? The Construct will be the location of the entrapment. Your men's task is to bring them all inside, including their god."

"How do you feel a god possessing a portion of yourself, does it bother you sometimes."

"Merging with my body, I have two souls, mine and his, I don't get any complaints, in fact, the first Fourth realm god swore to protect me, he respects what I do, but my mission to either protect, destroy or to take the Transcending could take place after finding the other Fourth realm, his twin. He (Thaniel) said after his twin took his 'sleep' the god in me has never seen him ever since."

"Maybe I can help." Said Elder Brother.

They pass through the gateway leaving the world of the Predator's kingdom, and there, Zenie/Thaniel stops to notice what's on the chamber's floor. The god Thaniel noticed something on the chamber ground, the ashes of a young boy he knew.

"Why is my dark aura surging?" My first time reacting to feeling a darker atmosphere around me, but not much dark that I needn't use a hunting ground view. I can feel Thaniel is mad, agitated, wanting to drag me somewhere. We run at super speed, BUT this time, too murky leading me his way.

We stop and knelt down looking at the ground, the dark shadow around subsided, and the three brothers came riding following us.

I can feel my eyes flooded with tears incessantly, and I could hear loud mind whispers of questions from the three brothers. It's started to annoy the god inside me!

"It's a graveyard of my younger twin brother, can't you see?!" Zenie's eyes turned dark, but the three brothers don't get why I am raging on my knee, instead of praying calmly. Thaniel in a despairing moment hit the graveyard so hard with his fist. No time speaking of what had truly transpired, hitting the ground that hard by a Fourth Realm can wake up resting souls who have witnessed what will happen to twin brother Haniel.

The atmosphere around the three brothers has turned the souls into a sequence of images of what had been done to Haniel by the Serpent god ordering his three female warriors to annihilate Haniel.

"But it's only Wednesday afternoon... the Serpent god, his apprentices, and whatever will happen on Friday hasn't taken place yet!?" Verified Elder Brother.

"You humans can never understand philosophies of gods; you live only at present times. The ancient never bestow ethereal concepts in you, I already saw what happened to my brother, the otherworldly vision is inescapable."

Thaniel read the inscription engraved on the rock, by their father through his Omni power. And on both margins were symbols itched by Thaniel, the sleeping buds.

"It should have been better if we both stay in one resurrected body, closer, always by your side. Anyway, there's Zenie, must be there a higher purpose that we need to merge with him, my brother."

Zenie's eyes blazed to silvery-white in front of the three freaking out Brothers. "What is it this time?" Brother Narija asked Elder Brother.

Before the brothers come to utter what to do next, Zenie has come to his senses, and spoke.

"There exists another Fourth Realm in the human world surface!" Elder Brother conceptualized the legend of the Twin Death god-brothers.

> "Go past the forever hidden...into the Fourth Realm
> Not any human nor ordinary god can handle,
> Respect the sleeping bud, under breezes or warmth.
> Forbidden to disturb or else you'll get crumble!"

Zenie has to hardly convince the Brothers especially the brain of the three, Elder Brother, and he's got one more left... "I'm not doing this for my own sake's transcendence...I know the vision of the god of this kingdom is with me, leading me on how to find to save both worlds. And my visions were his own messages. And that vision was accomplished by me, with the help of the strict command from a name he called himself the...never mind."

Zenie had been restricted beforehand not to disclose anything about *him*...the Fourth Realm during their encounter, a dark and malevolent one. The details accounting for the Fourth realm shouldn't and must not be heard of, spoken to, or seen by anyone human, or else the human will burn alive.

He remembers *him* said. "My existence alone in the human world can absolutely burn anyone in the distance, either with or without will. Merging with your body can defy that process, but your sensing of dangers and auras becomes futile. You become me, can see, smell, and feel the darkness in anyone...and we can get to the consciousness of others, that would make us fearsome to our opponents."

"Have you encountered the...?" Frightened to death to which Zenie has anticipated Elder Brother's quivering reaction. Elder Brother appeared trembling as he almost weakened to collapse, Brother Narija, in good assistance, supported him from behind.

Brother Zendre faces his own son, "who is this...this god?" (his father didn't dare to mention the Fourth realm).

Zenie discusses only... the warning inscription of the fortress gate.

"What does the warning say?" Elder Brother asked one more question because of one inference playing in his head.

Zenie looked at the old man, but without remorse, he's decided to utter just that to persuade them all. "It says...the gate, once opened, has served its purpose...accepting your risks."

Wednesday four-thirty dawn when they left Predator's kingdom. Riding each on their big black wolf, Thaniel darkened their presence by shadowing to hide from the public.

The look in the eyes of Elder Brother has altered to meddling amazement and confusion. And the discussion was carried over as deliberately insisted by Elder Brother in his other lab, located in one big chamber unit in the old basement of the city's library. It was five in the morning, the grandfather clock's bell sounded when it did alarm.

Elder Brother's grandfather was a shareholder of the library and the museum, inherited by him. It's a huge basement unit, owned by their family where his grandfather passed on to him all his secrets, shortcuts, research, and some crucial attribution of a few archaeologists.

"The legend is true. After you have mentioned the warning by the gate...the same warning is written by the heavy doors of the forbidden archives. This only means that there are two of them... because they were twin siblings who'd been specified to live within it. The Greeks myths called these twin sibling gods Thanatos and Hypnos."

Zenie did recoil in fear upon hearing Elder Brother saying the god's names. However, Zenie and the god within him heard the myth's silly name for the two Fourth Realm gods. That didn't count to bring out a curse to punish Elder Brother to be burned alive that very instant.

The interesting myths of the two twin brother gods continued to a past story of a sacred ritual when they were young and impulsive, that to gain more *Omnis (powers of the gods),* a ritual of 'Into thy Hands' must be solemnly conducted by any gods who wished to transcend. Any god must possess to offer three components of the realms in distress, showing that god must not overlook responsibilities regarding the welfare of the three realms (predators, deadly magic, and immortality). In response, the realms of the gods judge to reward the pleading god through a portal (the triangle of lights) a transcendence, in the form of a kingdom or sanctuary, a punishing weapon, and an Omni. And the judging gods before him said, **"take this all for things obligated to be done for what is due, that is to defend the less strength from those oppressors."**

But Elder Brother doesn't know anything about how the twin brothers were granted transcendence and why Thanatos' Fourth Realm and Hypnos' Fourth Realm are in different places. Then Elder Brother revealed a worn journal secured in a crafted wooden box; he opened up a page stapled with it a leather map of an excavation. On the next page was a black and white photograph of Marco polo holding in his hand the excavated object, a wall fragment showing a god kneeling before the judging gods and raising the 'triad symbol' of the realm gate of the Predator's Kingdom.

Finally, they magnified the held triad symbol and it seemed to show a rotating mechanical joint on both sides.

He pointed out some sketch resemblance that the triad symbol was a realm gate to Predator's kingdom. The two other realm gates of Deadly and Immortality can be bestowed only if the joints on the sides are mechanically altered. One will show the Greek symbol of death, or the omega, meaning the end...it's the realm gate referring to the Deadly magic. "That's why wizardry uses the hidden symbol of a crescent, which was derived from the shape of a scythe, not the moon." He drew the omega symbol on a piece of paper and folded it in the middle; his demo showed a picture of a scythe, a tool of a grim reaper. And lastly, in the Immortality kingdom, he drew a symbol of a fruit or a bud with sepals which are usually pointy like a 'W', but the middle point is somewhat enlarged. A different version of bud with sepal is the circle which means no end, and on top is the sepal, and its pedicel or peduncle. He turned the paper upside-down and elaborated on another culture (the Egyptian), and they both give the same meaning...the ankh, Egypt's symbol for immortality.

Without uttering words, god Zenie recalled a portion of his adventure into the Fourth realm, where he realized that god Thaniel, sitting on his throne, has the two axes/scythes embedded on the backrest when they aren't in use. And it took him to figure out just now that the two scythes and in between them is the pointy shape which holds the two scythes, form the three Symbols of the Realms.

"Give us a minute gentlemen," Zenie, in his blazing dark eyes, wanted to talk alone with Elder Brother. "Except you...Elder Brother."

"tell me, Elder Brother...no human can withstand the Omni strength, speed, and power of the collective (Forbidden archives).

With the terrified and astonishing reaction seen on the face of Elder Brother, he clarified Zenie's objective. "What do you mean, god Zenie?"

"Only I can complete the work to save my kingdom as well as your Brotherhood of Wisdom."

Zenie's voice and accent have changed to Thaniel's, his black aura magnified showing authority over any gods or gifted human from any of the three Realm kingdoms. "I'm not asking you to let me enter the Forbidden archives; I'm going in. And you will hear, see, or tell nothing... for you will not know anything...and I do not exist in your Brotherhood of Wisdom; therefore, I do not break any oath or conduct of the Brotherhood."

"I got frightened, shivered to my nerves in that fearsome power I perceived from Zenie's aura, but I knew it wasn't Zenie who just ordered me." Thaniel's aura subsided, and Zenie's eyes turned normal, seeing Elder Brother's eyes flowing with tears. He looked at the boy's sweet face, saying, "you promised god Zenie to keep this Wolf Brotherhood of Wisdom safe, please..."

And finally, Elder Brother said, "You better get into the Forbidden archives earlier tonight before the Congregation's Serpent realm god arrives by Friday."

Zenie has prowled into the Wisdom like hunting his prey with only his black streak of shadow but only to be noticed by some others as a slight breeze. Not even a single Congregation member or Elder Brother's followers have seen him sneak into. So, he waited down the mazy dungeon and further deeper he walked by the steel heavy double door with heavy door handles on both. And took a check out of how it looks. He read the sign, *"The door, once open, has served its purpose...your risks."* He recalled warning signs from the previous experience entering the Fourth realm back in the Predator's kingdom.

Every time Elder Brother visits the maze dungeon, a check out to the gate of the Forbidden archives requires him to come down once in a while. Even with a couple of assistance, a heavy steel door couldn't match to be opened by a single man or two, most unlikely to an elder like him.

Before Zenie had made a serious covenant to pursue his objective, he'd asked favor secretly from Elder Brother to exclude his father's presence upon entering alone into the Forbidden Archives.

"My vision does not complete a sense, and here I am inside the Forbidden archives. This all explains the missing point of my vision. The reason why the apex predator couldn't summon help was when his arm was devastated. Because *he* only represents the call of one realm."

After knowing what went wrong with the god predator in his dying situation, Zenie felt the agonizing god asking for another chance that he gave the effort to do the *calling.* His heart felt the agony too, he screamed out loud, with tears flowing. Infuriated!

The aura of the flaming wolf converges much more energy! Like he entered an arena of catacomb where he is the combustion, and the vast area is oxygen. That even the Omni strength, speed, and power from the many various archived (the collection of the forever hidden wisdom of the sleeping gently souls of the departed gifted Realm gods from the three kingdoms) were drawn to his flaming aura. The white aura of forbidden wisdom soared into a tsunami coming toward the center on him in the middle, and later became a tornado making him the eye of the storm of white aura of wisdom.

"Goram, your people and your Predator's kingdom will prevail and I will be the judge for that...this missing sense of sacrifice I cannot tolerate. But now that I am one Omni god, I will summon them...the true gate of the summon (the triangle light of the transcendence) will face me without staining my hands with blood of the three representative characters!"

"To err is not just human alone because everyone, including any World settler, starts from a tabula rasa!"

-Zenie, The Omni god

CHAPTER ELEVEN

THE TEN WOLF WARRIORS

Back to the current rendezvous of the ten wolf warriors of the Black Canis lupus, on the arrival of the three last wolf warriors, three of their comrades came out of the underground opening and asked them, "passwords?"

Hans, the leading, gets off his horse, steps forward, and states the passwords.... "Loyalty, bravery, truth, and freedom." And while reciting the passwords, his eyes skeptically explored to discover the three comrades in front of him were impostors. One of them must have a black locket to go in and out of the realm gate, but in his thought, the scoundrels are trying to trick them and steal their realm weapons. Chances are they would blend in with the rest and march with them, putting the life of the leader Elder Brother and his loyal friends in grave danger once the meeting at the cave takes place.

With their ability to mind talk in whispers, the power to have two-way or more communication at the encounter of enemies comes in at the ready. (Mind-whisper) "Sounds to me these three amateur deadly users are impostors; get ready to arm yourselves on my signal, Pike, and Zohr!!!"

The wolf warriors made a pact to challenge them with the discovered deception, pretending cleverly to add up as another way of the "physical password."

A keen observer and clever Hans smiled slightly. "With this duel of challenge, I may require each of us to draw our own realm weapons and fight with it, as a sign of our loyalty, bravery, truth, and freedom!" Hans and his comrades feel each others' augmented spirits as they stand up for themselves, more than ready as true Wolf warriors. Their fighting stance is extremely serious; ready to the death, they don't care as long as the deadly magicians fall on the ground first!

The three of them surge to draw their realm weapons, and with the power of alchemy to summon, instant heavy weapons emerge from their grips- one with a couple of axes, another with a bow and arrow, and one with a spear. Bold and agile they become when weapons from the realm tangibly materialize as their grips draw from unseen alchemy doors. Lust and greed for the death of their well-noticeable evil opponents, they bolted, setting aside the acts as the ordinary priesthood-preacher way Brothers characterize themselves inside the Wisdom. Full of exuberance, they engage in combat, but none of them ever speaks literally. It's their sharp mind who do the talking, like flying whispers as a mode of their conversations. Their raging on the attack as the scene took it in a slow-mo, the three of them executed the charging beautifully towards their opponents.

Gradually becoming of her image, Lucy steps forward to accept the challenge, "girls...enough of the bluff, they're pretending not to know we're impostors... show them how serpent warriors will grant their death wishes!"

Hans launches his spinning axe in a boomerang throw, too fast, Lucy couldn't dodge the attacking object, with the help of Cecilia's fast reflex, she turned Lucy into a log, transporting her to her side. While Jinx controls the spinning ax, she shifted its direction to the one with the spear. Instead, he blocks it. Pike fired his arrow at Jinx simultaneously, one was evaded by Jinx but the next one was right into her shoulder. Cecilia came to rescue Jinx by getting in her way. And with the power to cheat reality like the time, she heals to relieve Jinx's bleeding shoulder and faces the two simultaneous traversing arrows towards her. She levitated up a log and blocks them with it. And cast an alchemy circle where Pike stood, making his ground liquefied of her manipulation. Blinded by the enormous bright light from Lucy, Pike has lost balance and hit Hans with a shot. Although it didn't go through because of the armor. Lucy continued to unleash the blinding light but she was stopped when Zohr's launched his spear toward her. Lucy was thrown with broken ribs, as the slow-mo scene has shown it. Cecilia cast a clone of her and the three warriors ambush her with several attacks, but Cecilia was only buying time to save her injured comrades.

Came rushing outside from the underground opening, the other seven wolf warriors surrounded the three serpent warriors who fear nothing from them. Nobody knew the cornered serpent warriors were just clone manipulations, manipulated by the power of deception of mental projections. They took the chance to pass through the realm gate while it was open. Upon crossing the boundary successfully, the mind projection vanishes in thin air.

"Damn that spear warrior, I will see you bleed when I take my chances!" Lucy groaned in pain while Cecilia's healing her.

Everybody noticed all their weapons' inscribed markings glowing, "There's only one reason for this!" Reasoned the angered Hans, the chamber of the gateway was left open unguarded."

Zohr theorized. "We have no idea who they are but basing on their power to make a human construct means they are Deadly users."

"Deadly users from where?" Asked Pike.

Suzu filled in some explanations. "Elder Brother has mentioned only one thing to physically identify if a creature has bestowed himself a realm power system. Meaning... the creature's blood is darkened red, unlike humans on the surface world, we have bright red blood."

Pike recalled he had hit the shoulder of one of them. He picks up the blood-stained arrow and showed it to them for inspection.

"They're definitely human with borrowed power granted by realm deity or god, like us. It's red blood." Confirmed Suzu, "which means only one thing, we have congregation serpent warriors inside the kingdom."

Eleven in the evening. They all march back inside to the realm border into the Predator's kingdom, and they have to rush to the Howling wolf mountain before midnight, however on the course of their most strange journey, they were ambushed by three wolves. They are terribly enormous and appear to be disturbed from their territory as the men thought. A battle between three big wolves against ten wolf warriors with realm weapons is about to commence.

"Wait, has anyone observed they are the three black wolves that were on our side during the Wisdom trial?"

"I guessed not! They have no collars; they aren't the pets of Elder Brother!"

"Brave, loyalty, truth, and freedom..." Louder and louder, they chanted their dogma as they fully conjure all existing weapons to fiercely scare away the three creatures. But more from a distance behind the wolves were called to back up. Rushing towards dinner drooling as if they haven't devoured food for a week.

At the fight, the ten wolf warriors have been segregated into three groups, some men have incurred and have endured wound scratches, and others have sprained themselves, however, the wolves aren't as invincible as they were believed to be despite they put up a good fight, some of them were eliminated and vanished like dispersing flame ashes but something the warriors have found out after all of a sudden, the snarling wolves backed off, all together they withdraw and fled away as if someone called them. And two of the beasts got injured, barely running. One from the leg, another was battered by its side with a meteor hammer. The astonishing discovery was that the blood from those escaping beasts is red. "That's weird to perceive such an unsuited creature, why red blood?"

Suzu, the fastest swordsman warrior, deciphered the beasts that weren't from this kingdom. "They were clones, made out of deadly magic. From the three women, most probably!"

"So tenacious," Suzu whispered in fury. Men we gather in a pack, we march but we talk in mind whisper, stay focused...that's my order.

Among the ten warriors, seven have regrouped back together earlier than the rest. Worrying about the three who might have gone farther somewhere, two have arrived panting as they recounted they have heard them calling their names, and the last is waving at them although limping as he tries hard to nimble.

"What's the matter? Everyone here is present!" Ask Hans, the limping warrior using his other ax for support.

"We are all wondering here, how come these big wolves ooze red blood?" Suzu hinted as he scoured every gesture of Hans. However, he noted all is normal to Hans, especially the cool attitude even in a damn situation.

"Of course, red blood, see my axes, stain with their red blood!" Said Hans and laughed while soothing his sprained ankle.

"You don't get it. Creatures like them in this world obtain different components of elements, not even mentioning their humongous sizes and color...black." Suzu explained as he strongly disagrees with Hans'.

Opposing a story, the ax thrower named Hans narrated his theory based on a legend. "Ok, I have my theory on why some wolves still have the red blood in them...I grew up in England in the south; my great grandfather told me a story back when he was a teenager, black wolves were being hunted, and their government had resolved to end up amending laws regarding favoring to capture and the genocide of the black wolves. Legend says if it's the truth that one hunter saw a humongous black wolf... and the howling was strange as described by this hunter because he knew how the wolves around Midwest England and Wales' border calls for back up, this creature the big black wolf howls like he calls them to escape from the area. Until his theory has proven something, all wolves regardless of size and color have gone to extinction. He saw traces of footprints like thousands of them marched in the same direction. But the mystifying about his discovery was that footprints of thousand wolves had shown a bizarre discontinuity trail on the ground, as if erased, leading to nowhere."

"So, your great grandfather knew there was a portal in the forest of Midwest England...is that what you are saying? That these creatures originally came from our homeland." Suzu did a mind whisper to anyone who can hear him. *"Hans, you never mentioned any single about your great grandfather nor blood relative because you are adopted as a newborn and raised in the brotherhood."* And everyone who acknowledged that, smiled back at Suzu.

"They are aware of things like that but not as fortunate as us that we even cross the gate, and from our Elder Brother's wisdom, the name itself brings the story somewhat convincing, the gateway to the Predator's kingdom," Hans concluded the storytelling.

The ten warriors have recovered their strength and went back on their trek. Everyone has witnessed the aura emanating from the surface of the mountain. They have reached the site, the mountain that glows due to the aura of the creatures living on that mountain, resembling the howling wolf. One said, "it's beautiful!" Suzu just recalled what he just ordered them, no expression or talking, just mind whisper, and he glance to where it came from, Pike. He repeated, "mind whisper gentlemen! Because these impostors cannot hear us."

The truth is when humans roam any of the three realm kingdoms, only realm gods or someone endowed from the realm either by deliberation or unintentional can see a real aura or aura of manipulations both on the human world and the gods' realm.

Suzu, the only Asian realm warrior with the highest rank among the ten, recalled what Elder Brother told them about auras, *reiki*, or lifeforce in his homeland. Suzu spoke to them while at rest, facing all of them. "This is it, Elder Brother's intended final destination for us." And they all stood forming in a circle although the seven has noticed something awkward going on with the three: Hans, Pike, and Zohr. But from there, Cecilia has fixed it, he slowed the time of all the seven, so he could manipulate EVERYTHING in them. With the time reality manipulation, she's like moving all around them unseen! "The secret of the red gem!" She smirked and laughed like an evil, "with this power, I can enslave them all."

But there's one thing nobody knows about what the three suspected impostors did to the real black wolf warriors. They're the serpent warriors who shifted their images to the copied three victims, they've put them under a time spell, making their three victims' time reality at a very super slow pace. Remained trapped in that time reality manipulated by deadly magic, Hans, Pike, and Zohr could only be unleashed from the control of Cecilia when purged by a higher manipulator.

Why can't Jinx just kill the three victims? She remembers what realm god said to her during the baptism of their names, "if ever you want to kill... ask permission from me first..." Things like that play in her mind during the trekking. "So futile while I have the chance to turn them into mice." Jinx is frustratingly preoccupied.

Jinx continued to get upset with her god's rule. "Yeah, right...Serpent realm god, you are nowhere to be found. So where are you, and what's taking you so long to ambush? If only you were here, these ten wolf warriors could have been turned into ashes."

"Jinx, you better pipe all your senses down... and be advised that we cannot procure a steady mimicry if the body and soul of our sources are dead, understand?" Warned Lucy. "I can hear you from my distance. So don't you ever mess around; blend in nice and be quiet until we see the transcendence from the three kingdoms in action."

Cecilia joined their mind conversation, "I'm the one having much fun with my power among us three; I have deceived three of their members back in the dark forest under my time spell, and now I have the same idea when we get inside the cave mountain. So actually, cloning might be the best, magic clone for the rest, to create confusion."

As they walked inside the pitch-black tunnel, the gem torches supported by a carved caudron made of stone burned into flame as they all pass through their way. At the end of the tunnel, everyone assumed the result just greet them with an amazing appearance but instead, a dark abyss of space, and no clue to begin where to step on because a wide range of space darkness wouldn't assure them safety. They all stood there waiting...but one warrior (Lucy) pointed out something glistening... tiny stars twinkling and disappearing. Some twinkling lights move and stop.

Scanning to know the truth from not, Lucy steps forward even though she has not had the idea if she's walking onto some solid ground, but enough to wonder why her power to sustain her truth has no function in that chamber, the reason...there's nothing real in that chamber. No one was brave enough to step further except Lucy in the warrior disguise as the ax thrower (Hans). But before Lucy took one step, Suzu spoke to the ax thrower in mind-whisper, "be careful..." Suzu began to prove that the ax thrower wasn't him, for he hadn't obtained a response back from him. And the moment a foot landed on the ground; the gem bonfire burst into flame at the center of the huge circle of ground. The shimmering light through every structure of the remnants of the old city had caused wonders to everyones' awe. That made the pitch-black chamber as vast space inside the mountain appear intriguing upon their beholding. The burning gem of the bonfire in the middle cast shadows on the uneven ground, causing the obvious structure of one big circle marking underlying the thick dust from their far lookout. From his standpoint, Suzu has observed the long way to walk, starting from the irregular wide stone-carved stairs to the bridge, through the city wall, and lastly through the giant gate of another wall beyond that covers the transcending zone where the gem burns continuously soaring up high.

Warrior Pike (a clone and in the consciousness of Jinx) asks where the circled markings could be found in that wide area. And not only that, but they also must find at least three of them of the exact sizes.

"Why are we here? Summon to this place to search for the three big, circled markings? Although alchemy comprising science and medicine has something to do with these gateways, why not give us the specific coordinates to prepare it before the three wolf riders arrive? What's the use of spending time and more time searching for it? And what if we didn't find the three big, structured markings before they set foot inside? They must have a brilliant reason to allow us to find them."

Warrior Zohr (a clone and in the consciousness Cecilia) walked past Pike (Jinx) and said, "why not use what's inside your skull and not your mouth!" Warrior Zohr (Cecilia) stared at Jinx...and gestured to her with a flicking middle finger.

As they walked through the city proper, the major road ahead was blocked by large rubbles of a collapsed structure that seemed to bridge the gap between two towers across the road.

Hans (Lucy in disguise) signed them to stop and look for another way.

Zohr (Cecilia in disguise) suggested, "let's walk around and rendevous to that giant main gate." Pointed to the giant gate of the fortressed wall of the transcending zone.

Culminating due to paranoia of the wolf warriors' suspicion towards them, Cecilia's evil plan of creating confusion by replacing each remaining warrior with a clone slowly but definitely has come to a head. One at a time, with each one getting along with her, will turn apparently into her controlled clone, leaving behind all the copied and unconscious futile souls of warriors hidden somewhere in the remnant city. Enjoying the manifestation of control out of her deceptions, she's making the mind conversation with the other two serpent warriors in disguise. Finally, they march to rendezvous on the facade of the last gate.

Lucy communicates to Jinx her plot succeeded, "I've taken them all hostage...not only that, we all have the same will to crush down anyone who attempts to deviate from our objective."

Lucy came running with enormous joy as she approached Cecilia walking briskly with pride and setting forth her army. But looking around after head counting... "you missed one, Cecilia!" Specified Lucy.

"Really? Who?" Upset and annoyed and a bit embarrassed.

"The fastest and the smartest of them all, it's Suzu you overlooked," Lucy answered.

"No worries, warrior! Do not let frustration debilitates your strength and power. You are safe with me." With the power of Haniel, he healed him and rejuvenate all worn-out systemic structural Jinx crossed her arms, "never mind the smartest warrior, we're still complete, plus we have the clone army of realm warriors. I've no doubt you can make them more than a thousand heads.

Lucy intervenes. "And here's the good news... I've found what we came for; the floor we are standing on is one giant key to the triangle of light.

"Then...where are the other two?" Ask Jinx.

"Triangle of light...triangle." And she's starting to decipher as she looks sharp all around her and up above. Although the gem bonfire she assessed isn't offering much light to complete her quest, she added more brilliance to the burning gem. "*Fotizo!*" And the three look up. "Now that's the three keys that form the triangle. Exactly right!" Lucy smiled with intent.

She chanted, "Diaspora kryfis!" It was a greek term to mean dispersion of hiding...and all the three turned back to their actual images.

Suzu made up his mind to escape away from the hands of the three serpents.

After knowing I could not make use of any mind whisper to anyone, I presume I am the remaining uncontrolled among the pack. That alerted me to save myself against their deadly method. How did all got captured?

I was hiding, constantly moving, farther from the transcending zone into the forsaken city outside the protective high wall, but I feel a shadow moving wherever I go, and I quickly draw my sword from summoned alchemy door.

But I was stunned by how the shadow unarmed me, my quickest move to draw my sword was nothing compared to his disarming. The next thing I saw was that my sword was impaled into the solid brick ground halfway.

The shadow faces me, continuously flaming calmly its dark aura, my first time to see an aura so dark, and from there a boy revealed himself, walking in front of me in a hooded cloak. I remained quiet, glaring and observing.

"You need not worry, Suzu. I saw everything." He said... "I am the Mysterious hooded man, I am the god predator who evolved into Omni god predator, I am the boy who was about to leave my town, my city, and my family, the one true story narrated at the meeting assembly."

When I was getting my sword. He said, "I'd put it back." I didn't even notice how he did it.

They're both on top of the high protective wall that bound the entire vast transcending zone, just above the giant main gate. God Zenie is scheming a plan of actions, "so the circles of marking are connected, the base and two more others, forming its angle roof." From the observation of the scientific-minded Zenie, "what a megastructure device of space communication and gate built and hidden under the hollow mountain!"

Pretending, Suzu is not the type to be persuaded so easily. "I'm grateful Zenie that it was really, you." He stood up and abruptly draw his sword from manifested alchemy door. This time Zenie didn't interfere because he understands the warrior's subdued condition. He quickly asks the person a question related to his background, "Give me the exact name of your father, if you really are god Zenie!"

"Dr. Zendre Joshu."

"Where is he, brother Narija, and the Elder Brother?"

Hesitated to answer but he did it anyway, "they're all in the real Howling Wolf Mountain."

"So, this is a Construct?" The smart warrior Suzu started conceptualizing.

"Then what are we doing here? Making us your bait, well, you have succeeded, my men are already held, hostage! Hysterically explaining his side.

(Thaniel) **"This is why I hate involving myself with humans... their faces look adult, but their mind says otherwise."** And Thaniel even asks twin brother Haniel, "Could you make him sleep while we deal with the Serpents?"

(Haniel) **"Humans are humans, they utter many words, they complain many objections. Why...because they are limited!"**

"No worries, warrior! Do not let frustration debilitates your strength and power. You are safe with me." With the power of Haniel, he healed him and rejuvenate all worn-out systemic structural of his mind and body.

Omni Zenie observes...

Panning the caught scene to Cecilia, described by Thaniel as misleading, controls making more clones out of the six clone warriors. Hundreds of them aligned into formation.

The one lighting up the perimeter as if scouring the entire place is called the light-bringer, the female version of Lucifer, named Lucy.

Lucy called Cecilia, "I cannot use my power in the atmosphere. Don't know why?"

"You ask yourself; you answer yourself, who do we ask to answer our doubts and questions...you!" Cecilia responded logically.

Jinx who used to rely upon the ground to sustain her power, suggested, "why not use the ground, wider and concealed."

"And the youngest, disaster master...chaos and disorder." *Zenie conclusively described Jinx while burning the ground, even the plants that thrived for ages were burned down to create a thick wall of inferno between the giant main gate and the three of them.*

Jinx looks at her comrades and asks one thing. "Can I kill this time?"

"That's why she is the most nuisance!" Verified Suzu.

Finally, the three big wolves with the three riders have arrived! The despairing hope from Suzu's eyes had been quenched; his eyes emotionally flowed with tears. But opposite to what Suzu feels, the serpent warriors were filled with so much tension.

"Jinx and Cecilia...you know exactly we're outnumbered, but do you know that war is a game of mind either in force or in a truce? It's not that quantity that counts; it's the strategized plan of action; sometimes, deception matters the most. I will leave that to Cecelia to create confusion and fear among the enemy. I will act as the mind, Jinx...you will be my forces, to incapacitate or eliminate them, there's no difference!"

"Jinx...intensify the toxicity of the fire surrounding us! We must protect ourselves before *our* master arrives. Better if anyone resists to cross the infernal barrier, to show our enemy we intend to kill." The order came from Lucy as she stood in the middle and eventually levitated to observe around the perimeter and how Jinx modifies the common fire barriers into a *volcanic fire.*

The volcanic fire reflected in his eyes, Zenie reacted angrily, "My god me! That would entirely burn any creatures or human to the bones, despite the suffocating effect of the smoke once that fire barrier is crossed."

A *Volcanic fire* can only be found in the north of this entire land kingdom, where precipitation gets to the lowest pH when it reaches the ground. Too much accumulation of this acid goes to the melting point in the deep soil. And beneath the crust, that molten isn't ordinary...any creature who's no extreme defense for fire and ice would be annihilated instantly. But there's a good thing to this Volcanic fire when it reaches the ground surface after it dries up; it grows a magnanimous amount of the vegetation eaten by the Serpent dragons, the only predators that thrive there. And these creatures are one of the four predators that anyone hopes will not be encountered in any fight. They are also known as *volcanic fire-breathers*...and when they are cornered, they breathe out that Volcanic fire.

CHAPTER TWELVE

THE MIND, THE FORCE, AND THE DECEPTION

Then they (three wolves-riders) arrive and stop at the upper ground wherefrom below, the inferno sets in higher than before deliberately to block their way into the fully covered dirt circle marking, gazing at the three serpent warriors awaiting their next move. The looks of the riders in silhouette have belittled the still preparing opponents, underestimating. Witnessing the fearsome scenario and perceiving a pre-empt of their action, the big black wolves advance with glowed piercing eyes, slowly walking down the irregular stone carved stairway. And as they approached the level, the three black wolves began to pick up a running pace towards the bridge. Many black wolves, nearly a hundred, followed the three brothers raging onward to the battlefield, but beyond the huge heavy gate awaits the impending infernal death.

To give an extensive idea of what the huge circle marking looks like and what's it about, it's a horizon of eight miles by eight miles of evenly surface and two more of the same size that forms the apex of its roof. It is evidence of advanced intelligence-made, transfigured the inner ground of the huge mountain into a secret dormant gateway, a portal of space communication to convene a message from a summoner, and from there, either a response, support, or nothing would result from the summoning. Now the gods who once thrived there bestowed the norms and methods to their followers. Gradually, their populace has diminished that seems to have abandoned the place leaving structures of civilization remnants.

Before anyone could reach the vastness of the horizon of the circle of markings, a civilization (now ruins) must first be reached. And is divided by the main road connected by an arched bridge with the huge support of mechanicals in the middle. The bridge continued as its main path that goes through several gates: gate after the stairs, another gate before entering the town proper or its city, and after a mile, another massive, tall gate of the high wall, which on the other side reveals the horizon of the circle markings. Circle markings cannot be seen by anyone standing on it. At present, the horizon is abandoned and dark, even a considerable gem bonfire couldn't brighten up the entire triangulated ceiling.

Zenie's concern...

"That the three serpent warriors aren't as vulnerable as I and Suzu thought; they're more than prepared...just hiding all their secret weapons to bait the three riders to get closer."

The serpent warriors created a wall of fire to lure the three wolf riders, urging them to keep coming.

"These lady serpents are full of bluffs and smart, wanting their (male) opponents' ego to charge."

Wall of fire, despite serving as a distraction, is actually intensified into deadly. Besides, what's beyond that after crossing or jumping over is their ultimate method of destruction! I have perceived it ten steps ahead.

While seeing the riders getting nearer and nearer to the gate of the city, with the help of the twin gods, I dashed harder and faster to get to the three brothers to warn them; I did it in a black streak. With that physics-defying velocity, my surroundings seem to a halt.

"What was that?" The riders noticed.

"There goes again, a black streak." The Black wolf riders were Pike on the right lane, Hans in the middle, and Zohr on the left lane. Each leading riders have followers of the pack of wolves behind them and they go at a running pace. Running beside them, I necessitate to warn them of impending death.

But the riders couldn't decipher whether the entity in the dark aura is a friend or a foe. Because the gods within conceal my identity.

Haniel stretches the time longer, thus giving more time in a longer space before they could all reach the massive high gate baited with annihilating inferno.

"It's me...Zenie. Whatever you do...don't get through that last gate!"

The three riders were the original three wolf warriors (Hans, Pike, and Zohr) trapped by Cecilia's power, the time manipulation using the red Deadly gem had been destroyed. Hans began talking while on the move, "I am Elder Brother possessing the body of Hans, the warrior. I also allowed Brother Zendre, your father, and Brother Narija here to possess the consciousness of Pike and Zohr, respectively. We have rescued them from being time trapped in the woods."

"As of now, Zenie, our trancing bodies are in tranquility inside the real howling wolf mountain. Nobody knows we are there. So, what do you have for us, (Omni) god predator Zenie?"

"Don't you insist to get to the middle, or more of your wolf allies will die? I had warned you!"

I led and ran ahead. "Let the left rider turn left, and the right rider turn right!!"

Elder Brother yelled, he couldn't do mind-whisper with god Zenie. "Do you have a plan?" That yell could be heard, but the twin gods of the Fourth Realm occupied most of me and by the speed of the pack of black wolves behind Elder Brother, I envisioned the death of the Black wolves, stampeding and squeezing and burning.

"If only the twin gods haven't possessed me, I could guarantee to lead them... this is vazey! Many will die!"

"I must improvise! With the twin gods' power (Thaniel's devastation to smash down the entire high gates of two big blocks, Haniel's creation, to turn the rubles of the gate into lush vegetations) I will certainly save more lives!"

Just to avert the envisioned death, I tripled my speeding dash towards the gate, smashing the entire thick two blocks of huge rock gates. Ram!!!

Continuously Elder Brother went through the smashed gate, but god Zenie, deciphering Elder Brother was unknowingly leading his pack of wolves to death. He obstructed by lifting Elder Brother's wolf and him disregarding the impact of their fall, but the pack of wolves behind continued to run, mitigated the impact by growing vegetation, some others continued to the Volcanic fire, and it was too late, and outside the gate, others stampeded by the bridge and fell. Zenie saw how Haniel helped the dying creatures to 'sleep' and take out their pain, as he extracted their souls quickly.

"Bloody death..."

A slow motion of agony twirl around me in my upsetting moment, seems like my enemies the serpents are winning.

However, Lucy and Jinx, as the defense lead, the two serpent warriors have clearly felt the presence of the god Thaniel.

"Jinx, does it ring a bell to you? He's here."

Lucy perceived me as Thaniel in a power from a god surrounded by a dark aura, and they've got something for me (as Thaniel). Soaring vigorously by inviting more souls of the darkness to leverage my aura, they caught me off-guard!

"By the power of these bright lights, levitating, you…the darkest creature, will vanish and be blinded forever!" They were papers with small markings, while Lucy whispers the oration, the papers' writing ignited as they levitate and form an alchemy circle, panning the view from above, Thaniel is the center. After the oration, Lucy's eyes flame as well as the papers in blinding lights; all the same time synchronized lightning strikes Thaniel.

Thaniel scream and was thrown into the quick-burning volcano fire.

With that strong burst of lightning, the possession of the body and mind by the twin gods disperse from me. Swallowed entirely by the volcanic fire, I roared the loudest, Cecilia, preparing a thousand armies further back, looked alarmed at the reckoning roar, long and echoing inside the hollow mountain. Even the black wolf pack slowed down.

While Lucy and Jinx continued to celebrate an early presumed victory. Evilly smiling at each other, "that is just the beginning!" They both saw how the entire pack discontinue and by the look at the beast, they stand down.

I was all covered with a burning flame, and there was no scream of agony, but a lowly growl and snarl came. The continuous burning...has turned into a golden aura that intensifies the burning! There is movement in the Volcanic fire. It has consumed my superficial skin but didn't die. I roared while inside the fire, I am calling my people!

Everyone recognized my burning golden aura... my red flaming eyes stand out.

I walk out of the fire unharmed! "My turn!"

Lucy glared at the creature, "that's beyond belief Jinx, what kind of creature have we encountered?!"

"You mutt serpents!"

Finally, I felt intertwined heightening emotions of anguish and power!

Looking in wrathful gaze at his three opponents who were gazing back at him, reacted with fear. Zenie's aura burst the second time so powerfully, that the aura reached beyond miles of the triad megastructure!

"Bloody shame...what kind of monster is he?" Jinx got annoyingly infuriated by her volcanic fire that usually disintegrates flesh and bones, but it didn't work out as it was supposed to.

Jinx turned to Lucy. "Not even a slight shred of his flesh got torn out by your bolt, Lucy!"

"Cecilia, who the hell have we encountered here??" Lucy asks.

"I thought you were Lucy...you're supposed to inform me, not ask me!"

Vampire wolf Zenie snarled back and uttered.

"I'm your predator responding to my preys who just made foolish show-up mistakes! A proof that you all three are below me. You should not have brought sources of light when I'm around! Now, you're dead squirming serpents."

He stood and roared loudly...the fire barricade extinguished, the sound wave frequency of his roar converges and spread outward...

"I will call more of my people to join this fight against you serpents! **You're not even predator enough to fight us to the death, there's no turning back from this kingdom!"**

In the kingdom territory of the Vampire wolves, their red eyes responded, and sniffing to where the roar of the Vampire wolf god originated. All clans of

Vampire wolves: both hunters and soldiers who were saved by god Zenie before as a sacrifice to the Fourth realm, now became allies to the summoning god.

They all left and vanished in zap and swoosh...and showed up quickly within a minute, occupying different areas of the transcending zone.

Zenie must buy a few more minutes, as he draws more heat from the extinguished fire barricades until all the red molten solidifies totally, leaving just enough heat to turn the incoming clan into Vampire wolves.

Igniting into flame, all burn and shred their charred skin, growling and snarling, and terrifyingly emerged the pack of the Vampire wolves only the god of the Vampire wolf can give an order.

The thousand clone warriors made by Cecilia were all ready, grunting and moving their weapons up high. Cecilia has upgraded his army, knowing that the incoming and preparing people of the predator god are unarmed. She has assured that her clone warriors are protected with extra copied realm weapons dispersed in mid-air that is now levitating, steady, and will be launched by hand manipulation of Cecilia. To specify, long spears are on the frontline, countless axes are above them, and several rows of stretched bows with arrows are aligned in the back. All extra realm weapons are levitating, a plan of action controlled under Cecilia's synchronized will.

However, half an hour earlier, before the three serpent warriors acknowledge the appearance of their assets, the three black wolves' riders, Lucy seems uncomfortable with only thousands of clone army.

"Aren't you glad I've contributed army to do our burden, about you? The things you've set up above, would they work to hold them back?"

Why not spit it out!? Order me for more requests, rather than making some insulting remarks that three of *us* can perceive. Stupid mind!"

"Cecilia...don't start a fight! I know what she meant by that!!!" Jinx just yelled to call her attention.

But Cecilia, the older among the three, just wanted a little respect but instead obtained an insult; got provoked to ignite a fight with whoever would like to put her down.

Yelling consequently occurred; their auras aggravated.

"I don't want to reveal them...aren't you using your senses? Now, who is more stupid? We are about to start a war." Loudly uttered Lucy to Cecilia.

Jinx sided Lucy. "War is supposed to be *keeping your best cards* from the intelligence of your opponents. But, and vice versa, war can also mean sneaking and stealing their plans...intelligence."

Hearing the line *keeping your best cards* just made her become belittled, then furious. "Don't you dare lecture me; I've trained so hard, and I stood out among other candidates who are known to be more ahead of me, skillful and fiercer in sorcery before you were both introduced to the Congregation. Who among my colleagues during the training and elimination test has emerged to the top without a single scratch...nobody but me, most of them dead...some wounded, friends included!" Her eyes shed tears.

Cecilia continued, facing Lucy. "You must be good, rather excellent in plotting and in the architecture of war plans, and Jinx...the most indispensable when it comes to synchronized forces. But I hate to say this, who aided you when you both ran out of tactics...I always decide plan B, making sure my comrades survive.

Lucy crossed her arms; took a deep breath. "Well, thanks for that assurance. Hmm, without your deadly, what are you, Cecilia?"

"I'm stamina, a fast reflex, stubborn will, and a closed contact fighter. Compared to you without deadly, **you're just a plan but no action."** Cecilia smirked.

Jinx yelled. "Hey, enough of that useless arguments! We aren't enemies with each other!"

"You too, young brat. If you really are serious about appeasing the two of us, do not side with anyone! You're always impulsive and very emotional. **You're an action without rational thinking!"**

Jinx's perception has darkened; Cecilia's statements are precise to her observation. And Jinx's tantrum escalated... she cast a spell to make Cecilia, who's only a couple of meters away, become a stone. Cecilia hardened from the feet, slowly climbing to the upper body, and as they both saw the spell set the trachea of Cecilia, she barely could breathe and gasped for air.

Following the turning into stone, Jinx simultaneously manifested a gateway from the ground, an alchemy circle brightening as one opened for a terrifying creature to leap up.

Robust and bearded dark bull humanoid in form carrying a single, but double-bladed ax showed up. The *ax minotaur* strikes hard the stone figure of Cecilia diagonally, resulting in rubbles.

"What have you done...you..." And Lucy shook her head; she could read Jinx's sudden change of emotion. Guilt, anger, and dread.

Jinx got terrified that she was on her knees, shaking, whimpering; she knew with her uncontrolled violent anger, she'd killed Cecilia. Projecting her rage, she turned the ax minotaur, too, into stone. "Raaaahhh!!!" She shouted in an anguished.

"Whatever the arguments, ladies...we are in this together...to work it out." The voice is familiar. From a distance, poor visibility comes walking not one Cecilia but three Cecilias, and each spoke the line.

"How'd you escape that deadly magic?" Lucy came closer.

"Simple, our thoughts are just one and all connected, despite being segregated. Whatever anyone among us has in mind, we all share it." Cecilia continued.

"Right now, I can tell that you have an additional plan, a change of plan based on what you saw from Jinx's deadly magic on me...ah correction... on myself clone."

"Everything happens for a reason. Before, I admit I looked down on you, Cecilia. Your method of war, the deception, and distraction are part of war too, and are dangerous."

She turned to Jinx bringing up her spirit. "Her expertise in this system of tactics benefits the war for us, buying time and creating chaos in their mind." Lucy elaborated.

Cecilia still saw Jinx crying on the ground; she assessed her she needed to be comforted. "Jinx...come here." Offered her hand to Jinx and hugged her. The young serpent warrior apologized and asked a favor; although she felt embarrassed at the absurd moment, Jinx whispered something, and tears are still flowing.

"If ever we can't make it to win this war, I beg you...don't leave me behind, Cecilia."

"I promise to you this...three of us will live. Win or lose."

CHAPTER THIRTEEN

FOUR AGAINST FOUR

Elder Brother saw how Zenie's people arrived courageously and with loyalty as they aligned behind him. And all the Vampire wolf clan draw the fire that Zenie has, sharing (one to another) the same flame, moving like a wave until they burn to transform into monsters of real Vampire wolves. Then, finally, he saw how just the big guys of the clan of the Vampire wolves changed their bodies into broad, robust, and angry Vampire wolves after shedding off their burned skin. Then, like normal house dogs, after a water bath, they shake off their charred skin.

Hundreds of them roared, howled, and snarled as they ran toward the army of cloned warriors. But the black wolves led and instructed by Elder Brother, waited on both sides of the clone army, where nobody has noticed them running forth because they have blended into the darkest far side of the circle marking. The clones have advanced toward the Vampire wolves, who were focused on the charging predators without awareness of the movement of the Black wolves infiltrating from both sides.

The Black wolves are fierce, they aren't from the human world, but Elder Brother has used the infamous *Circe magic*. It is the enchantment to alter humans into monsters or alter ferocious beasts to take obedience. The magic originated from goddess Circe, adept at enchantment or sorcery of converting characteristics involving humans to animals, and animals for compliance.

But the three serpent warriors never left their stance and waited...and waited more and let the Vampire wolves come closer. Finally, the point has been reached, and wickedly, the three serpent warriors look at each other, "it's time!!!"

Ax minotaurs leap from the ground with the several portals created by Jinx, but to the surprise, the bold and fearless ax-slashing monsters seem to come out of nowhere. Although slow but many, the tactic was more terrifying when Cecilia added more deceptions of fake portals.

The twin gods in dark and light consciousness have no one to possess to let their consciousness in, and they both cannot take the long irritating nuisance caused by the war.

"We got to move and join in twin brother," demanded Thaniel.

"We have to settle these warring idiots either by peace or force, brother Thaniel," Haniel replied as he scoured for a body to possess.

"Absolutely by force, Han," Thaniel suggested.

Thaniel, the god of death and darkness, has spotted Zohr, surrounded by clone warriors; when seeing the lady serpent Jinx is on her way to warrior Zohr, Thaniel decided, it's best for him to possess Zohr and to face Jinx.

Finally, Haniel, the god of sleep death, and peace has found one, Pike, while in action stretching and aiming his arrow at more or less ten cloned warriors to expose Cecilia from behind. "Let me teach you how to fight even when you ran out of those arrows." And he merges into Pike's body.

Now, the previous swapped-out consciousness returned to Brother Zendre and Brother Narija in the Howling wolf mountain, which awakened them from their trances, both sitting on crossed legs beside Elder Brother.

Brother Zendre, pondering with doubts, asks Brother Narija, who also happens to be awakened. "What happened to us there in the battle?"

Brother Narija described how he was being kicked out of the body and mind by another consciousness. "I had a feeling a higher god pushed me out, so easily. The consciousness threatened to devour my consciousness leaving my true body and mind to become vegetables if I don't leave entirely!"

"And you?" He asked Brother Zendre.

"I saw a bright diamond-like figure engulf me; he politely nodded at me to take the body and mind, while looking at me in the eyes sharply and firmly." Answered Brother Zendre.

When Pike (consciousness of Haniel) ran out of his arrow, he jumped off from his black wolf and knelt for a few secs, he turned asleep, and his eyes had gone shiny bright white when he opened them up. At the moment of bolting in straight to anyone on the way, white static surrounds him, and specks of dirt spread out (in slow mo)! All took a decapitating slash. Cecilia has observed him with his eyes closed, not even literally facing his enemies. Haniel or Han has the power to fight better when he's calm asleep; his consciousness is more receptive, fully awake, and ahead of steps when fully close to one focus.

Zohr (consciousness of Thane or Thaniel), on the other hand, must spreads out dark energy that sucks in evilness from all enemies, to weaken them and surrender, until Jinx has only been the last opponent standing. Cecilia and Jinx collaborated. Creating a distracting portal where Thaniel could see them, he stopped looking around for comrades, saving them and taking them away from portals (fake).

But the real portal of brightening appeared further back where nobody could notice. Griffins came out flying, and Thaniel yelled and looked at Hans (consciousness of Elder Brother) and Zenie to warn them that enemies were coming fast from behind.

Surprised by the whiplash, Hans (Elder Brother) was captured by the griffin's claws, which elevated him in mid-air, but he uses his ax to cut the legs off. He landed safely with a hero stance, but he landed in front of the three serpent warriors. The three serpent warriors gaze at him, and abruptly Jinx opens a portal, bigger than those before. And it manifested beneath Hans.

The brightening portal cracked open, and a wild snake dragon sprang out. It doesn't have wings, but it's long, a serpent dragon they call, and it's one of the four terrifying predators in the kingdom located in the north. Hans was tossed by the snout of the creature and ready to be eaten, but Hans threw his left ax directly, striking the eye. He landed on the back of the neck using the other ax. Then, he boomerangs the right ax and maneuvers the beast to where the ax returns. A big slash hits the beast's throat.

Haniels' ahead-of-time senses are making him desperately dull and slow.

"I wish I could manipulate to turn the whole vicinity into my sanctuary, the Fourth Realm; I'm swifter and smoother when colliding head-to-head with several enemies."

Haniel, still in sleeping mode, consciously saw Jinx as responsible for procuring those circle gateways. So, he burst into several after images, launching himself like a projectile towards every griffin, accompanied by multiple lightning bolts and white streaks, and all the flying griffins have turned out falling, wing feathers scattered around.

"Did I get your attention?" Haniel, in godlike, landed with the sharp sword outstretched by his side.

It has gotten into Lucy's nerves, and her disappointment made her furious, "Jinx, I need you to bring three serpent dragons under *Circe* spell at the same time, and I want you to fry that white bolting god!!"

"I will create three bright orbs that will follow the bolting god and let your serpent dragon focus on those orbs. Then, once the orb catches him, you simultaneously let your serpent dragons breathe out the tremendous volcanic fire on him."

The chase has continued for a while. In compliance, the serpent dragons go round and round, but many creatures suffer already from both sides due to the collateral damage the colossal beasts have caused. The spewing of a real serpent dragon's volcanic fire is the only killing weapon the Vampire wolves cannot go against...except god predator Zenie.

From the Elder Brother's command, he ran towards and briefed Zenie with something new. They are talking side by side while trying to seclude the deadliest of the three, Cecilia.

"Collaborate with the god of darkness, and use the Hunting ground view of your people, hurry!!!"

"I have to overthrow this deception warrior first, not as threatening but the cleverest, and her last resort, escapade."

Zenie vanishes in thin air, (the plan to leave Elder Brother in Han's body) but Zenie asks one big favor from Elder Brother, to use the aura of creation, changing his image to another but with the instruction of the Omni Zenie.

"Follow my lead, Elder Brother."

Elder Brother using Deadly, vanishes and emerges, but this time when the dark mist had dissipated, there were two Zenies in front of Cecilia.

"Now I get it...you want to play...I think I've seen you before, you were in that house of the doctor...hmm, Dr. Joshu. We were there, you thought you hug and kiss your mom, but it's a deception I made..."

While explaining that to the two Zenies, there were no real Zenies in both. Those were the aura of creations of Elder Brother and him altering the image of Hans into one Zenie and a human construct. But where is the real Zenie? The Omni Zenie. He's been moving non-stop on an Omni speed that no Deadly user can see while listening to Cecilia's chat.

Cecilia made two mimics of her, too.

And the attack started from the two Zenies...when the four did their rumbles, backflip, and vanishing and emerging, scratching with claws... the Omni Zenie watching in unseen speed, instructed Elder Brother to switch one Zenie vampire wolf into another Cecilia. Using Cecilia as a puppet, Elder Brother (as the remaining Zenie) whispered a deadly spell to attach all inflictions to the two Cecilia on whatever was done to the puppet Cecilia.

The puppet Cecilia listens to what is whispered by Zenie the Elder Brother in disguise. Puppet Cecilia came closer from the back and grab choke Zenie (acting). The table has turned, and Cecilia and her mimic were both confused.

With a swift escape from the grab, Zenie the disguise held both hands of the puppet Cecilia by his deeply immersed claws and did a backflip to break them, while both Cecilias who were confused suffered the same arm fractures and deep wound scratches. When Zenie the disguise was about to snatch the heart through the chest of doomed puppet Cecilia, the Omni Zenie in slow mo saw the escaping real Cecilia from the clone in shadow form.

Zenie the disguise, flaunted the heart of puppet Cecilia lifted, pumping its remaining heartbeats.

"You're dead clever Cecilia." Yelling to distract the two other Serpent warriors.

To expose the weakness, Omni Zenie in image after image slowed down to be noticed by escaping Cecilia eye to eye as he humiliates her that he was not in the fight the entire time, that the Zenie has turned back into the body and image of Hans. **"You knew that you could have been dead if the real god predator was in the fight."**

The previous plan of Elder Brother had been complied with...

Omni Zenie summoned Thaniel...as the hazy black figure left Zohr, Zenie carefully brought the woozy warrior to safety. But before the hazy dark figure of Thaniel, which is the consciousness, comes in contact with Zenie's mind, Thaniel asks him a question.

"Why just now when a lot of your people have suffered?" From the question alone, Thaniel has an intelligent and decisive way to put an end to the enemies. But Zenie asked himself, "why didn't you (Thaniel) finish me off in your sanctuary, back in the Fourth Realm?"

"This isn't an excuse Thaniel, but our foes have brought through the portal the very equal monster my clan ever has. And I NEED YOU to darken the whole ground...that's my request."

Zenie with the god within grew black raven wings and soar around in circle image after image until the place darkened. Zenie landed as a god with the black lightning bolts, and his eyes glowed the luminaire eyes for the Hunting ground view.

Zenie soared again to lead all Vampire wolves, even the wounded, of course only the Vampire wolves can see him converging all his people for one purpose.

Zenie, with the power of Thaniel, gave the wounded and his dying people a dark revision. A death power that gives back weaken body a push to revive a consciousness by rejuvenating its destroyed body parts.

"The serpent dragon cannot see a thing in this ground. With the god as my friend, all I want is our ground and our people not to be taken over by any predator...because only one king predator prevails in this kingdom, the Vampire wolves."

"Thaniel helped me turn the ground into the Fourth Realm but temporarily to defeat the serpent dragon under Circe's magic. No foes nor beasts under Circe's spell can annihilate you... because they're all blind when it's time to use our Hunting ground view."

The serpent dragons, blinded by the total darkness, have no choice but to fire up their breaths. Now the Vampire wolves can attack all at once, and one serpent dragon is down, swarmed to be easily preyed on by Black wolves and Vampire wolves. Zenie ended it by ramming the head of the dragon and smashing its head so hard against the ground, "for my allies and my people that you've destroyed!"

Haniel saw one serpent dragon face to face. For the many who can tell and who can see including the gazing serpent dragon, Haniel seems to freeze in front of it, and the giant beast breathes out its fire.

"You're too slow; I have impaled you already before you realize right beneath your lower jaw. And your fire breath has reached me, but it's my after-image. And for the record and for the many, I never freeze. How can I? I'm asleep..."

I then dissolve the darkness. Elder Brother in the body of Hans called the two, Zohr and Pike. And I landed, telling Thaniel to take Zohr's and Haniel to Pike's. The four of them face the remaining standing enemies before their eyes.

Panning to their frontline, from Elder Brother (Hans), down to Zenie god, Thaniel (Zohr), and Haniel (Pike) gaze at the remaining foes from their distance...the serpent dragon, Jinx, Cecilia, and Lucy.

There's too much tension, horribly dreadful, and devastating. Piercing and gazing eyes against each other, auras emerging in full, overlapping whispers of thoughts as means of communications among comrades, in each group, of plans and tactics, diversions and confusions, all in arrays of war of both remaining best of the deadliest.

The two sides have witnessed one last paper bomb falling as it swayed lightly to a direction that seem to lead down to a stoned figure of once a creature, the ax minotaur. The two opposing groups sensed the falling paper bomb and understood upon collision and resulting in an explosion of the stone figure, that would set them to charge on to their final battle!

EPILOGUE

This is a peek at the following sequences and future consequences during the war and after it.

"Do not overlook yourself Elder Brother, mind only your soul...heal it even before harm can strike you...Thaniel and Haniel will never forsake Zohr's and Pike's for the twin brothers have infinite souls, spared through times." That was the reminder Omni Zenie has hinted for he knew the beast Serpent dragon can trample on anything melting even the hardest object created both on earth and on the kingdom, but what about an object that is made in between both worlds? Does Elder Brother know of anything created in between both worlds in existence?

Elder Brother was left alone with the Serpent dragon, while the three have taken action to isolate each of themselves together with their respective match opponents by opening another gate.

As the battle between Elder Brother and the beast continues, energies dwindle, all being used to heal himself, thus, the construct mimic of the Howling Mountain fades into thin air, disclosing the actual location of the mountain. Notifying the clever entrapment, even made Sira, the Serpent god wilder and angrier, as he charged on with the armies of mercenaries to the exposed mountain.

Unfortunately, they were stopped by Suzu and his comrades, the six other Wolf warriors.

Sira spoke with aggressiveness and arrogance, "You call yourself army against my mercenaries? Even a no-brainer human knows what this match could lead to each of you! Shall I say you need a clear steer of your senses to guide you in your future direction?"

From out of nowhere, a flash of red streak stops as a mist and materialized into a woman figure farther behind the seven wolf warriors, suited in the armor of the Vampire wolf, the god queen predator. She looks up straight ahead to Sira furiously, "**I am their future direction!**"

ACKNOWLEDGMENTS

"No man is an entire island."

Thank you so much Tellwell Talent, Inc. and to my Project Manager Jerrard Ivan Dulce, his crew members, to Mary Apple B., and to Von as my book cover designer.

Special thanks are given to the following friends and colleagues for contributing to sketching images as artists and character models: Paul and his son, Team leader Crystal, Emily, and Amanda, Steph, Scott, and Team leader Jacob.

Dedicated this Passion and Talent I finally
accomplished in memory of
Grandfather Silvestre U.
and
my Father Jose R. De Leon

ABOUT THE AUTHOR

Cladennis D. is a supernatural and fantasy afficionado. His eldest cousin inspired him by his enthusiasm for Superman (Christopher Reeve), which led him to do drawings of anime and manga at young age, preferably the action combat moves and poses.

Canadian filmmaker James Cameron's works and ideas with archaelogist Simcha J. and the Zecharia Sitchin's published writings invigorated him to start writing and self-publishing his first fiction novel, The Predators' Kingdom: Into the Gateway.

He is currently at work on the next Predators' Kingdom series: The Secrets of Alfa.

CPSIA information can be obtained
at www.ICGtesting.com
Printed in the USA
LVHW101336031222
734486LV00010B/545/J